QUEEN OF THE MARTIAN CATACOMBS

An Eric John Stark Adventure

BY

LEIGH BRACKETT

VERTVOLTA PRESS
REDISCOVERY
Edition

Book and Cover Design: Vladimir Verano, VertVolta Design

ISBN: 978-1-60944-105-0

VERTVOLTA PRESS

vvdesignpress@gmail.com

www.vertvoltapress.com

Other Eric John Stark Adventures
from VertVolta Press

BLACK AMAZON OF MARS

ENCHANTRESS OF VENUS

SINUS MERIDIANI
SINUS SABAEUS
SYRTIS MAJOR PLANITIA
HELLAS PLANITIA

TOPIA PLANITIA
ELYSIUM
PLANITIA
SIDIS
ANITIA
CERBER
HESPERIA
PLANUM
ELYSIUM
PLANITIA

FOR HOURS THE HARD-PRESSED BEAST HAD FLED ACROSS THE Martian desert with its dark rider. Now it was spent. It faltered and broke stride, and when the rider cursed and dug his heels into the scaly sides, the brute only turned its head and hissed at him. It stumbled on a few more paces into the lee of a sandhill, and there it stopped, crouching down in the dust.

The man dismounted. The creature's eyes burned like green lamps in the light of the little moons, and he knew that it was no use trying to urge it on. He looked back, the way he had come.

In the distance there were four black shadows grouped together in the barren emptiness. They were running fast. In a few minutes they would be upon him.

He stood still, thinking what he should do next. Ahead, far ahead, was a low ridge, and beyond the ridge lay Valkis and safety, but he could never make it now. Off to his right, a lonely tor stood up out of the blowing sand. There were tumbled rocks at its foot.

"They tried to run me down in the open," he thought. "But here, by the Nine Hells, they'll have to work for it!"

He moved then, running toward the tor with a lightness and speed incredible in anything but an animal or a savage. He was of Earth stock, built tall, and more massive than he looked by reason of his leanness. The desert wind was bitter cold, but he did not seem to notice it, though he wore only a ragged shirt of Venusian spider silk, open to the waist. His skin was almost as dark as his black hair, burned indelibly by years of exposure to some terrible sun. His eyes were startlingly light in colour, reflecting back the pale glow of the moons.

With the practised ease of a lizard he slid in among the loose and treacherous rocks. Finding a vantage point, where his back was protected by the tor itself, he crouched down.

After that he did not move, except to draw his gun. There was something eerie about his utter stillness, a quality of patience as unhuman as the patience of the rock that sheltered him.

The four black shadows came closer, resolved themselves into mounted men.

They found the beast, where it lay panting, and stopped. The line of the man's footprints, already blurred by the wind but still plain enough, showed where he had gone.

The leader motioned. The others dismounted. Working with the swift precision of soldiers, they removed equipment from their saddle-packs and began to assemble it.

The man crouching under the tor saw the thing that took shape. It was a Banning shocker, and he knew that he was not going to fight his way out of this trap. His pursuers were out of range of his own weapon. They would remain so. The Banning, with its powerful electric beam, would take him—dead or senseless, as they wished.

He thrust the useless gun back into his belt. He knew who these men were, and what they wanted with him. They were officers of the Earth Police Control, bringing him a gift—twenty years in the Luna cell-blocks.

Twenty years in the grey catacombs, buried in the silence and the eternal dark.

He recognised the inevitable. He was used to inevitables—hunger, pain, loneliness, the emptiness of dreams. He had accepted a lot of them in his time. Yet he made no move to surrender. He looked out at the desert and the night sky, and his eyes blazed, the desperate, strangely beautiful eyes of a creature very close to the roots of life, something less and more than man. His hands found a shard of rock and broke it.

The leader of the four men rode slowly toward the tor, his right arm raised.

His voice carried clearly on the wind. "Eric John Stark!" he called, and the dark man tensed in the shadows.

The rider stopped. He spoke again, but this time in a different tongue. It was no dialect of Earth, Mars or Venus, but a strange speech, as harsh and vital as the blazing Mercurian valleys that bred it.

"Oh N'Chaka, oh Man-without-a-tribe, I call you!"

There was a long silence. The rider and his mount were motionless under the low moons, waiting.

Eric John Stark stepped slowly out from the pool of blackness under the tor.

"Who calls me N'Chaka?"

The rider relaxed somewhat. He answered in English, "You know perfectly well who I am, Eric. May we meet in peace?" Stark shrugged. "Of course."

He walked on to meet the rider, who had dismounted, leaving his beast behind. He was a slight, wiry man, this EP C officer, with the rawhide look of the frontiers still on him. His hair was grizzled and his sun-blackened skin was deeply lined, but there was nothing in the least aged about his hard good-humoured face nor his remarkably keen dark eyes.

"It's been a long time, Eric," he said.

Stark nodded. "Sixteen years." The two men studied each other for a moment, and then Stark said, "I thought you were still on Mercury, Ashton."

"They've called all us experienced hands in to Mars." He held out cigarettes. "Smoke?"

Stark took one. They bent over Ashton's lighter, and then stood there smoking while the wind blew red dust over their feet and the three men of the patrol waited quietly beside the Banning. Ashton was taking no chances. The electro-beam could stun without injury.

Presently Ashton said, "I'm going to be crude, Eric. I'm going to remind you of some things."

"Save it," Stark retorted. "You've got me. There's no need to talk about it."

"Yes," said Ashton, "I've got you, and a damned hard time I've had doing it. That's why I'm going to talk about it."

His dark eyes met Stark's cold stare and held it.

"Remember who I am—Simon Ashton. Remember who came along when the miners in that valley on Mercury had a wild boy in a cage, and were going to finish him off like they had the tribe that raised him. Remember all the years after that, when I brought that boy up to be a civilised human being."

Stark laughed, not without a certain humour. "You should have left me in the cage. I was caught a little old for civilising."

"Maybe. I don't think so. Anyway, I'm reminding you," Ashton said.

Stark said, with no particular bitterness, "You don't have to get sentimental. I know it's your job to take me in."

Ashton said deliberately, "I won't take you in, Eric, unless you make me." He went on then, rapidly, before Stark could answer. "You've got a twenty-year sentence hanging over you, for running guns to the Middle-Swamp tribes when they revolted against Terro-Venusian Metals, and a couple of similar jobs.

"All right. So I know why you did it, and I won't say I don't agree with you. But you put yourself outside the law, and that's that. Now you're on your way to Valkis. You're headed into a mess that'll put you on Luna for life, the next time you're caught."

"And this time you don't agree with me."

"No. Why do you think I near broke my neck to catch you before you got there?" Ashton bent closer, his face very intent. "Have you made any deal with Delgaun of Valkis? Did he send for you?"

"He sent for me, but there's no deal yet. I'm on the beach. Broke. I got a message from this Delgaun, whoever he is, that there was going to be a private war back in the Drylands, and he'd pay me to help fight it. After all, that's my business."

Ashton shook his head.

"This isn't a private war, Eric. It's something a lot bigger and nastier than that. The Martian Council of City-States and the Earth Commission are both in a cold sweat, and no one can find out exactly what's going on. You know what the Low-Canal towns are—Valkis, Jekkara, Barakesh. No law-abiding Martian, let alone an Earthman, can last five minutes in them. And the back-blocks are absolutely verboten. So all we get is rumours.

"Fantastic rumours about a barbarian chief named Kynon, who seems to be promising heaven and earth to the tribes of Kesh and Shun—some wild stuff about the ancient cult of the Ramas that everybody thought was dead a thousand years ago. We know that Kynon is tied up somehow with Delgaun, who is a most efficient bandit, and we know that some of the top criminals of the whole System are filtering in to join up. Knighton and Walsh of Terra, Themis of Mercury, Arrod of Callisto Colony—and, I believe, your old comrade in arms, Luthar the Venusian."

Stark gave a slight start, and Ashton smiled briefly.

"Oh, yes," he said. "I heard about that." Then he sobered. "You can figure that set-up for yourself, Eric. The barbarians are going to go out and fight some kind of a holy war, to suit the entirely unholy purposes of men like Delgaun and the others.

"Half a world is going to be raped, blood is going to run deep in the Drylands—and it will all be barbarian blood spilled for a lying promise, and the carrion crows of Valkis will get fat on it. Unless, somehow, we can stop it."

He paused, then said flatly, "I want you to go on to Valkis, Eric— but as my agent. I won't put it on the grounds that you'd be doing civilisation a service. You don't owe anything to civilisation, Lord knows. But you might save a lot of your own kind of people from getting slaughtered to say nothing of the border-state Martians who'll be the first to get Kynon's axe.

"Also, you could wipe that twenty-year hitch on Luna off the slate, maybe even work up a desire to make a man of yourself, instead of a sort of tiger wandering from one kill to the next." He added, "If you live."

Stark said slowly, "You're clever, Ashton. You know I've got a feeling for all planetary primitives like those who raised me, and you appeal to that."

"Yes," said Ashton, "I'm clever. But I'm not a liar. What I've told you is true."

Stark carefully ground out the cigarette beneath his heel. Then he looked up. "Suppose I agree to become your agent in this, and go off to Valkis. What's to prevent me from forgetting all about you, then?"

Ashton said softly, "Your word, Eric. You get to know a man pretty well when you know him from boyhood on up. Your word is enough."

There was a silence, and then Stark held out his hand. "All right, Simon—but only for this one deal. After that, no promises." "Fair enough." They shook hands.

"I can't give you any suggestions," Ashton said. "You're on your own, completely. You can get in touch with me through the Earth Commission office in Tarak. You know where that is?"

Stark nodded. "On the Dryland Border."

"Good luck to you, Eric."

He turned, and they walked back together to where the three men waited. Ashton nodded, and they began to dismantle the Banning. Neither they nor Ashton looked back, as they rode away.

Stark watched them go. He filled his lungs with the cold air, and stretched. Then he roused the beast out of the sand. It had rested, and was willing to carry him again as long as he did not press it. He set off again, across the desert.

The ridge grew as he approached it, looming into a low mountain chain much worn by the ages. A pass opened before him, twisting between the hills of barren rock.

He traversed it, coming out at the farther end above the basin of a dead sea. The lifeless land stretched away into darkness, a vast waste of desolation more lonely even than the desert. And between the sea-bottom and the foothills, Stark saw the lights of Valkis.

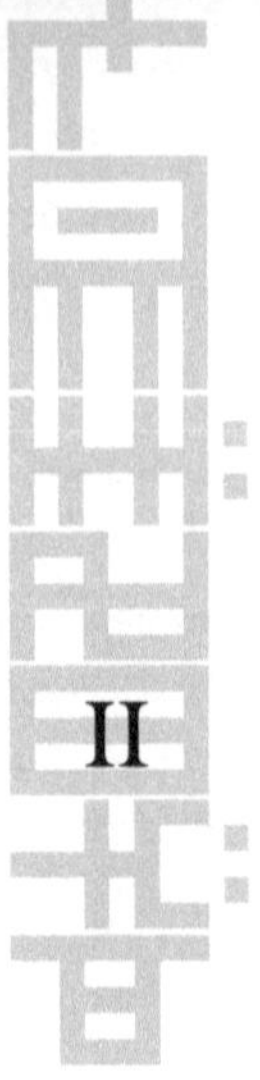

II

There were many lights, far below. Tiny pinpricks of flame where torches burned in the streets beside the Low-Canal—the thread of black water that was all that remained of a forgotten ocean.

Stark had never been here before. Now he looked at the city that sprawled down the slope under the low moons, and shivered, the primitive twitching of the nerves that an animal feels in the presence of death.

For the streets where the torches flared were only a tiny part of Valkis. The life of the city had flowed downward from the cliff-tops, following the dropping level of the sea. Five cities, the oldest scarcely recognisable as a place of human habitation. Five harbours, the docks and quays still standing, half buried in the dust.

Five ages of Martian history, crowned on the topmost level with the ruined palace of the old pirate kings of Valkis. The towers still stood, broken but indomitable, and in the moonlight they had a sleeping look, as though they dreamed of blue water and the sound of waves, and of tall ships coming in heavy with treasure.

Stark picked his way slowly down the steep descent. There was something fascinating to him in the stone houses, roofless and silent in the night. The paving blocks still showed the rutting of wheels where carters had driven to the marketplace, and princes had gone by in gilded chariots. The quays were scarred where ships had lain against them, rising and falling with the tides.

Stark's senses had developed in a strange school, and the thin ve-neer of civilisation he affected had not dulled them. Now it seemed to him that the wind had the echoes of voices in it, and the smell of spices and fresh-spilled blood.

He was not surprised when, in the last level above the living town, armed men came out of the shadows and stopped him.

They were lean, dark men, very wiry and light of foot, and their faces were the faces of wolves—not primitive wolves at all, but beasts of prey that had been civilised for so many thousands of years that they could afford to forget it.

They were most courteous, and Stark would not have cared to disobey their request.

He gave his name. "Delgaun sent for me."

The leader of the Valkisians nodded his narrow head. "You're ex-pected." His sharp eyes had taken in every feature of the Earthman, and Stark knew that his description had been memorised down to the last detail. Valkis guarded its doors with care.

"Ask in the city," said the sentry. "Anyone can direct you to the palace."

Stark nodded and went on, down through the long-dead streets in the moonlight and the silence.

With shocking suddenness, he was plunged into the streets of the living.

It was very late now, but Valkis was awake and stirring. Seeth-ing, rather. The narrow twisting ways were crowded. The laughter of women came down from the flat roofs. Torchlight flared, gold and scarlet, lighting the wineshops, making blacker the shadows of the alley-mouths.

Stark left his beast at a serai on the edge of the canal. The pad-docks were already jammed. Stark recognized the long-legged brutes of the Dryland breed, and as he left a caravan passed him, coming in, with a jangling of bronze bangles and a great hissing and stamping in the dust.

The riders were tall barbarians—Keshi, Stark thought, from the way they braided their tawny hair. They wore plain leather, and their blue-eyed women rode like queens.

Valkis was full of them. For days, it seemed, they must have poured in across the dead sea bottom, from the distant oases and the barren deserts of the back-blocks. Brawny warriors of Kesh and Shun, making holiday beside the Low-Canal, where there was more water than any of them had seen in their lives.

They were in Valkis, these barbarians, but they were not part of it. Shouldering his way through the streets, Stark got the peculiar flavour of the town, that he guessed could never be touched or changed by anything.

In a square, a girl danced to the music of harp and drum. The air was heavy with the smell of wine and burning pitch and incense. A lithe, swart Valkisian in his bright kilt and jewelled girdle leaped out and danced with the girl, his teeth flashing as he whirled and postured. In the end he bore her off, laughing, her black hair hanging down his back.

Women looked at Stark. Women graceful as cats, bare to the waist, their skirts slit at the sides above the thigh, wearing no ornaments but the tiny golden bells that are the peculiar property of the Low-Canal towns, so that the air is always filled with their delicate, wanton chiming.

Valkis had a laughing, wicked soul. Stark had been in many places in his life, but never one before that beat with such a pulse of evil, incredibly ancient, but strong and gay.

He found the palace at last—a great rambling structure of quarried stone, with doors and shutters of beaten bronze closed against the dust and the incessant wind. He gave his name to the guard and was taken inside, through halls hung with antique tapestries, the flagged floors worn hollow by countless generations of sandalled feet.

Again, Stark's half-wild senses told him that life within these walls had not been placid. The very stones whispered of age-old violence, the shadows were heavy with the lingering ghosts of passion.

He was brought before Delgaun, the lord of Valkis, in the big central room that served as his headquarters.

Delgaun was lean and catlike, after the fashion of his race. His black hair showed a stippling of silver, and the hard beauty of his face was strongly marked, the lined drawn deep and all the softness of youth long gone away. He wore a magnificent harness, and his eyes, under fine dark brows, were like drops of hot gold.

He looked up as the Earthman came in, one swift penetrating glance. Then he said, "You're Stark."

There was something odd about those yellow eyes, bright and keen as a killer hawk's yet somehow secret, as though the true thoughts behind them would never show through. Instinctively, Stark disliked the man.

But he nodded and came up to the council table, turning his attention to the others in the room. A handful of Martians—Low-Canallers, chiefs and fighting men from their ornaments and their proud looks—and several outlanders, their conventional garments incongruous in this place.

Stark knew them all. Knighton and Walsh of Terra, Themis of Mercury, Arrod of Callisto Colony—and Luhar of Venus. Pirates, thieves, renegades, and each one an expert in his line.

Ashton was right. There was something big, something very big and very ugly, shaping between Valkis and the Drylands.

But that was only a quick, passing thought in Stark's mind.

It was on Luhar that his attention centred. Bitter memory and hatred had come to savage life within him as soon as he saw the Venusian.

The man was handsome. A cashiered officer of the crack Venusian Guards, very slim, very elegant, his pale hair cropped short and curling, his dark tunic fitting him like a second skin.

He said, "The aborigine! I thought we had enough barbarians here without sending for more."

Stark said nothing. He began to walk toward Luhar.

Luhar said sharply, "There's no use in getting nasty, Stark. Past scores are past. We're on the same side now."

The Earthman spoke, then, with a peculiar gentleness.

"We were on the same side once before. Against Terror-Venus Metals. Remember?"

"I remember very well!" Luhar was speaking now not to Stark alone, but to everyone in the room. "I remember that your innocent barbarian friends had me tied to the block there in the swamps, and that you were watching the whole thing with honest pleasure. If the Company men hadn't come along, I'd be screaming there yet."

"You sold us out," Stark said. "You had it coming."

He continued to walk toward Luhar.

Delgaun spoke. He did not raise his voice, yet Stark felt the impact of his command.

"There will be no fighting here," Delgaun said. "You are both hired mercenaries, and while you take my pay you will forget your private quarrels. Do you understand?"

Luhar nodded and sat down, smiling out of the corner of his mouth at Stark, who stood looking with narrowed eyes at Delgaun.

He was still half blind with his anger against Luhar. His hands ached for the kill. But even so, he recognised the power in Delgaun.

A sound shockingly akin to the growl of a beast echoed in his throat. Then, gradually, he relaxed. The man Delgaun he would have challenged. But to do so would wreck the mission that he had promised to carry out here for Ashton.

He shrugged, and joined the others at the table. Walsh of Terra rose abruptly and began to prowl back and forth.

"How much longer do we have to wait?" he demanded. Delgaun poured wine into a bronze goblet. "Don't expect me to know," he snapped. He shoved the flagon along the table toward Stark.

Stark helped himself. The wine was warm and sweet on his tongue. He drank slowly, sitting relaxed and patient while the others smoked nervously or rose to pace up and down. Stark wondered what, or who, they were waiting for. But he did not ask.

Time went by.

Stark raised his head, listening. "What's that?"

Their duller ears had heard nothing, but Delgaun rose and flung open the shutters of the window near him.

The Martian dawn, brilliant and clear, flooded the dead sea bottom with harsh light. Beyond the black line of the canal a caravan was coming toward Valkis through the blowing dust. It was no ordinary caravan. Warriors rode before and behind, their spearheads blazing in the sunrise. Jewelled trappings on the beasts, a litter with curtains of crimson silk, barbaric splendour. Clear and thin on the air came the wild music of pipes and the deep-throated throbbing of drums.

Stark guessed without being told who it was that rode out of the desert like a king.

Delgaun made a harsh sound in his throat. "It's Kynon, at last!" he said, and swung around from the window. His eyes sparkled with some private amusement. "Let us go and welcome the Giver of Life!"

Stark went with them, out into the crowded streets. A silence had fallen on the town. Valkisian and barbarian alike were caught now in a breathless excitement, pressing through the narrow ways, flowing toward the canal.

Stark found himself beside Delgaun in the great square of the slave market, standing on the auction block, above the heads of the throng. The stillness, the expectancy of the crowd were uncanny ...

To the measured thunder of drums and the wild skirling of desert pipes, Kynon of Shun came into Valkis.

III

Straight into the square of the slave market the caravan came, and the people pressed back against the walls to make way for them. Stamping of padded hooves on the stones, ring and clash of harness, brave glitter of spears and the great two-handed broadswords of the Drylands, with drumbeats to shake the heart and the savage cry of the pipes to set the blood leaping. Stark could not restrain an appreciative thrill in himself.

The advance guard reached the slave block. Then, with deafening abruptness, the drummers crossed their sticks and the pipers ceased, and there was utter silence in the square.

It lasted for almost a minute, and then from every barbarian throat the name of Kynon roared out until the stones of the city echoed with it.

A man leaped from the back of his mount to the block, standing at its outer edge where all could see, his hands flung up. "I greet you, my brothers!"

And the cheering went on.

Stark studied Kynon, surprised that he was so young. He had expected a grey-bearded prophet, and instead, here was a brawny-shouldered man of war standing as tall as himself.

Kynon's eyes were a bright, compelling blue, and his face was the face of a young eagle. His voice had deep music in it—the kind of voice that can sway crowds to madness.

Stark looked from him to the rapt faces of the people—even the Valkisians had caught the mood—and thought that Kynon was the most dangerous man he had ever seen. This tawny-haired barbarian in his kilt of bronze-bossed leather was already half a god.

Kynon shouted to the captain of his warriors, "Bring the captive and the old man!" Then he turned again to the crowd,urging them to silence. When at last the square was still, his voice rang challengingly across it.

"There are still those who doubt me. Therefore I have come to Valkis, and this day—now!—I will show proof that I have not lied!"

A roar and a mutter from the crowd. Kynon's men were lifting to the block a tottering ancient so bowed with years that he could barely stand, and a youth of Terran stock. The boy was in chains. The old man's eyes burned, and he looked at the boy beside him with a terrible joy.

Stark settled down to watch. The litter with the curtains of crimson silk was now beside the block. A girl, a Valkisian, stood beside it, looking up. It seemed to Stark that her green eyes rested on Kynon with a smouldering anger.

He glanced away from the serving girl, and saw that the curtains were partly open. A woman lay on the cushions within. He could not see much of her, except that her hair was like dark flame and she was smiling, looking at the old man and the naked boy. Then her glance, very dark in the shadows of the litter, shifted away and Stark followed it and saw Delgaun. Every muscle of Delgaun's body was drawn taut, and he seemed unable to look away from the woman in the litter.

Stark smiled very slightly. The outlanders were cynically absorbed in what was going on. The crowd had settled again to that silent, breathless tension. The sun blazed down out of the empty sky. The dust blew, and the wind was sharp with the smell of living flesh.

The old man reached out and touched the boy's smooth shoulder, and his gums showed bluish as he laughed.

Kynon was speaking again.

"There are still those who doubt me, I say! Those who scoffed when I said that I possessed the ancient secret of the Ramas of long ago—the secret by which one man's mind may be transferred into another's body. But none of you after today will doubt that I hold that secret!

"I, myself, am not a Rama." He glanced down along his powerful frame, half-consciously flexing his muscles, and laughed.

"Why should I be a Rama? I have no need, as yet, for the Sending-on of Minds!"

Answering laughter, half ribald, from the crowd.

"No," said Kynon, "I am not a Rama. I am a man like you. Like you, I have no wish to grow old, and in the end, to die." He swung abruptly to the old man.

"You, Grandfather! Would you not wish to be young again—to ride out to battle, to take the woman of your choice?"

The old man wailed, "Yes! Yes!" and his gaze dwelt hungrily upon the boy.

"And you shall be!" The strength of a god rang in Kynon's voice. He turned again to the crowd and cried out.

For years I suffered in the desert alone, searching for the lost secret of the Ramas. And I found it, my brothers! I hold their ancient power. I alone—in these two hands I hold it, and with it I shall begin a new era for our Dryland races!

"There will be fighting, yes. There will be bloodshed. But when that is over and the men of Kesh and Shun are free from their ancient bondage of thirst and the men of the Low-Canals have regained their own—then I shall give new life, unending life, to all who have followed me. The aged and lamed and wounded can choose new bodies from among the captives. There will be no more age, no more sickness, no more death!"

A rippling, shivering sigh from the crowd. Eyeballs gleaming in the bitter light, mouths open on the hunger that is nearest to the human soul.

"Lest anyone still doubt my promise," said Kynon, "watch. Watch—and I will show you!"

They watched. Not stirring, hardly breathing, they watched.

The drums struck up a slow and solemn beat. The captain of the warriors, with an escort of six men, marched to the litter and took from the woman's hands a bundle wrapped in silks. Bearing it as though it were precious beyond belief, he came to the block and lifted it up, and Kynon took it from him.

The silken wrappings fluttered loose, fell away. And in Kynon's hands gleamed two crystal crowns and a shining rod.

He held them high, the sunlight glancing in cold fire from he crystal.

Behold!" he said. "The Crowns of the Ramas!"

The crowd drew breath then, one long rasping Ah!

The solemn drumbeat never faltered. It was as though the pulse of the whole world throbbed within it. Kynon turned. The old man began to tremble. Kynon placed one crown on his wrinkled scalp, and the tottering creature winced as though in pain, but his face was ecstatic.

Relentlessly, Kynon crowned with the second circlet the head of the frightened boy.

"Kneel," he said.

They knelt. Standing tall above them, Kynon held the rod in his two hands, between the crystal crowns.

Light was born in the rod. It was no reflection of the sun. Blue and brilliant, it flashed along the rod and leaped from it to wake an answering brilliance in the crowns, so that the old man and the youth were haloed with a chill, supernal fire.

The drumbeat ceased. The old man cried out. His hands plucked feebly at his head, then went to his breast and clenched there. Quite suddenly he fell forward over his knees. A convulsive tremor shook him. Then he lay still.

The boy swayed and then fell forward also, with a clashing of chains.

The light died out of the crowns. Kynon stood a moment longer, rigid as a statue, holding the rod which still flickered with blue lightning. Then that also died.

Kynon lowered the rod. In a ringing voice he cried, "Arise, Grandfather!"

The boy stirred. Slowly, very slowly, he rose to his feet. Holding out his hands, he stared at them, and then touched his thighs, and his flat belly, and the deep curve of his chest.

Up the firm young throat the wondering fingers went, to the smooth cheeks, to the thick fair hair above the crown. A cry broke from him.

With the perfect accent of the Drylands, the Earth boy cried in Martian, "I am in the youth's body! I am young again!"

A scream, a wail of ecstasy, burst from the crowd. It swayed like a great beast, white faces turned upward. The boy fell down and embraced Kynon's knees.

Eric John Stark found that he himself was trembling slightly. The Valkisian wore a look of intense satisfaction under his mask of awe. The others were almost as rapt and open-mouthed as the crowd.

Stark turned his head slightly and looked down at the litter. One white hand was already drawing the curtains, so that the scarlet silk appeared to shake with silent laughter.

The serving girl beside it had not moved. Still she looked up at Kynon, and there was nothing in her eyes but hate.

After that there was bedlam, the rush and trample of the crowd, the beating of drums, the screaming of pipes, deafening uproar. The crowns and the crystal rod were wrapped again and taken away. Kynon raised up the boy and struck off the chains of captivity. He mounted, with the boy beside him. Delgaun walked before him through the streets, and so did the outlanders.

The body of the old man was disregarded, except by some of Kynon's barbarians who wrapped it in a white cloth and took it away.

Kynon of Shun came in triumph to Delgaun's palace. Standing beside the litter, he gave his hand to the woman, who stepped out and walked beside him through the bronze door.

The women of Shun are tall and strong, bred to stand beside their men in war as well as love, and this red-haired daughter of the Drylands was enough to stop a man's heart with her proud step and her white shoulders, and her eyes that were the colour of smoke. Stark's gaze followed her from a distance.

Presently in the council room were gathered Delgaun and the outlanders, Kynon and his bright-haired queen—and no other Martians but those three.

Kynon sprawled out in the high seat at the head of the table. His face was beaming. He wiped the sweat off it, and then filled a goblet with wine, looking around the room with his bright blue eyes.

"Fill up, gentlemen. I'll give you a toast." He lifted the goblet. "Here's to the secret of the Ramas, and the gift of life!"

Stark put down his goblet, still empty. He stared directly at Kynon.

"You have no secret," said Stark deliberately.

Kynon sat perfectly still, except that, very slowly, he put his own goblet down. Nobody else moved.

Stark's voice sounded loud in the stillness.

"Furthermore," he said, "that demonstration in the square was a lie from beginning to end."

IV

STARK'S WORDS HAD THE EFFECT OF AN ELECTRIC SHOCK ON THE listeners. Delgaun's black brows went up, and the woman came forward a little to stare at the Earthman with profound interest.

Kynon asked a question, of nobody in particular. "Who," he demanded, "is this great black ape?"

Delgaun told him.

"Ah, yes," said Kynon. "Eric John Stark, the wild man from Mercury." He scowled threateningly. "Very well—explain how I lied in the square!"

"Certainly. First of all, the Earth boy was a prisoner. He was told what he had to do to save his neck, and then was carefully coached in his part. Secondly, the crystal rod and the crowns are a fake. You used a simple Purcell unit in the rod to produce an electronic brush discharge. That made the blue light. Thirdly, you gave the old man poison, probably by means of a sharp point on the crown. I saw him wince when you put it on him."

Stark paused. "The old man died. The boy went through his sham. And that was that."

Again there was a flat silence. Luhar crouched over the table, his face avid with hope. The woman's eyes dwelt on Stark and did not turn away.

Then, suddenly, Kynon laughed. He roared with it until the tears ran.

"It was a good show, though," he said at last. "Damned good. You'll have to admit that. The crowd swallowed it, horns, hoof and hide."

He got up and came round to Stark, clapping him on the shoulder, a blow that would have laid a lesser man flat.

"I like you, wild man. Nobody else here had the guts to speak out, but I'll give you odds they were all thinking the same thing."

Stark said, "Just where were you, Kynon, during those years you were supposed to be suffering alone in the desert?"

"Curious, aren't you? Well, I'll let you in on a secret." Kynon lapsed abruptly into perfectly good colloquial English. "I was on Terra, learning about things like the Purcell electronic discharge."

Reaching over, he poured wine for Stark and held it out to him. "Now you know. Now we all know. So let's wash the dust out of our throats and get down to business."

Stark said, "No."

Kynon looked at him. "What now?"

"You're lying to your people," Stark said flatly. "You're making false promises, to lead them into war."

Kynon was genuinely puzzled by Stark's anger. "But of course!" he said. "Is there anything new or strange in that?"

Luhar spoke up, his voice acid with hate. "Watch out for him, Kynon. He'll sell you out, he'll cut your throat, if he thinks it best for the barbarians."

Delgaun said, "Stark's reputation is known all over the system. There's no need to tell us that again."

"No." Kynon shook his head, looking very candidly at Stark. "We sent for you, didn't we, knowing that? All right."

He stepped back a little, so that the others were included in what he was going to say.

"My people have a just cause for war. They go hungry and thirsty, while the City-States along the Dryland Border hog all the water sources and grow fat. Do you know what it means to watch your children die crying for water on a long march, to come at last to the oasis and find the well sanded in by a storm, and go on again, trying to save your people and your herd? Well, I do! I was born and bred in the Drylands, and many a time I've cursed the border states with a tongue like a dry stick.

"Stark, you should know the workings of the barbarian mind as well as I do. The men of Kesh and Shun are traditional enemies. Raiding and thieving, open warfare over water and grass. I had to give them a rallying point—a faith strong enough to unite them. hem. Resurrecting the Rama legend was the only hope I had.

"And it has worked. The tribes are one people now. They can go on and take what belongs to them—the right to live. I'm not really so far out in my promises, at all. Now do you understand?"

Stark studied him, with his cold cat-eyes. "Where do the men of Valkis come in—the men of Jekkara and Barakesh? Where do we come in, the hired bravoes?"

Kynon smiled. It was a perfectly sincere smile, and it had no humour in it, only a great pride and a cheerful cruelty.

"We're going to build an empire," he said softly. "The City-States are disorganised, too starved or too fat to fight. And Earth is taking us over. Before long, Mars will be hardly more than another Luna.

"We're going to fight that. Drylander and Low-Canaller together, we're going to build a power out of dust and blood—and there will be loot in plenty to go round."

"That's where my men come in," said Delgaun, and laughed. "We low-Canallers live by rapine."

"And you," said Kynon, "the hired bravoes," are in it to help. I need you and the Venusian, Stark, to train my men, to plan campaigns, to give me all you know of guerrilla fighting. Knighton has a fast cruiser. He'll bring us supplies from outside. Walsh is a genius, they tell me, at fashioning weapons. Themis is a mechanic, and also the cleverest thief this side of hell—saving your presence, Delgaun! Arrod organised and bossed the Brotherhood of the Little Worlds, which had the Space Patrol going mad for years. He can do the same for us. So there you have it. Now, Stark, what do you say?"

The Earthman answered slowly, "I'll go along with you—as long as no harm comes to the tribes."

Kynon laughed. "No need to worry about that."

"Just one more question," Stark said. "What's going to happen when the people find out that this Rama stuff is just a myth?"

"They won't," said Kynon. "The crowns will be destroyed in battle, and it will be very tragic, but very final. No one knows how to make more of them. Oh, I can handle the people! They'll be happy enough, with good land and water."

He looked around then and said plaintively, "And now can we sit down and drink like civilised men?"

They sat. The wine went round, and the vultures of Valkis drank to each other's luck and loot, and Stark learned that the woman's name was Berild.

Kynon was happy. He had made his point with the people, and he was celebrating. But Stark noticed that though his tongue grew thick, it did not loosen.

Luhar grew steadily more morose and silent, glancing covertly across the table at Stark. Delgaun toyed with his goblet, and his yellow gaze which gave nothing away moved restlessly between Berild and Stark.

Berild drank not at all. She sat a little apart, with her face in shadow, and her red mouth smiled. Her thoughts, too, were her own secret. But Stark knew that she was still watching him, and he knew that Delgaun was aware of it.

Presently Kynon said, "Delgaun and I have some talking to do, so I'll bid you gentlemen farewell for the present. You, Stark, and Luhar—I'm going back into the desert at midnight, and you're going with me, so you'd better get some sleep."

Stark nodded. He rose and went out, with the others.

An attendant showed him to his quarters, in the north wing. Stark had not rested for twenty-four hours, and he was glad of the chance to sleep.

He lay down. The wine spun in his head, and Berild's smile mocked him. Then his thoughts turned to Ashton, and his promise. Presently he slept, and dreamed.

He was a boy on Mercury again, running down a path that led from a cave mouth to the floor of a valley. Above him the mountains rose into the sky and were lost beyond the shallow atmosphere. The rocks danced in the terrible heat, but the soles of his feet were like iron, and trod them lightly. He was quite naked.

The blaze of the sun between the valley walls was like the shining heart of Hell. It did not seem to the boy N'Chaka that it could ever be cold again, yet he knew that when darkness came there would be ice on the shallows of the river. The gods were constantly at war.

He passed a place, ruined by earthquake. It was a mine, and N'Chaka remembered dimly that he had once lived there, with several white-skinned creatures shaped like himself. He went on without a second glance.

He was searching for Tika. When he was old enough, he would mate with her. He wanted to hunt with her now, for she was fleet and as keen as he at scenting out the great lizards.

He heard her voice calling his name. There was terror in it, and N'Chaka began to run. He saw her, crouched between two huge boulders, her light fur stained with blood.

A vast black-winged shadow swooped down upon him. It glared at him with its yellow eyes, and its long beak tore at him. He thrust his spear at it, but talons hooked into his shoulder, and the golden eyes were close to him, bright and full of death.

He knew those eyes. Tika screamed, but the sound faded, everything faded but those eyes. He sprang up, grappling with the thing …

A man's voice yelling, a man's hands thrusting him away. The dream receded. Stark came back to reality, dropping the scared attendant who had come to waken him.

The man cringed away from him. Delgaun sent me. He wants you—in the council room." Then he turned and fled.

Stark shook himself. The dream had been terribly real. He went down to the council room. It was dusk now, and the torches were lighted.

Delgaun was waiting, and Berild sat beside him at the table. They were alone there. Delgaun looked up, with his golden eyes.

"I have a job for you, Stark," he said. "You remember the captain of Kynon's men, in the square today?"

"I do."

"His name is Freka, and he's a good man, but he's addicted to a certain vice. He'll be up to his ears in it by now, and somebody has to get him back by the time Kynon leaves. Will you see to it?"

Stark glanced at Berild. It seemed to him that she was amused, whether at him or at Delgaun he could not tell. He asked,

"Where will I find him?"

"There's only one place where he can get his particular poison— Kala's, out on the edge of Valkis. It's in the old city, beyond the lower quays." Delgaun smiled. "You may have to be ready with your fists, Stark. Freka may not want to come."

Stark hesitated. Then, "I'll do my best," he said, and went out into the dusky streets of Valkis.

He crossed a square, heading away from the palace. A twisting lane swallowed him up. And quite suddenly, someone took his arm and said rapidly.

"Smile at me, and then turn aside into the alley."

The hand on his arm was small and brown, the voice very pretty with its accompaniment of little chiming bells. He smiled, as she had bade him, and turned aside into the alley, which was barely more than a crack between two rows of houses.

Swiftly, he put his hands against the wall, so that the girl was prisoned between them. A green-eyed girl, with golden bells braided in her black hair, and impudent breasts bare above a jewelled girdle. A handsome girl, with a proud look to her.

The serving girl who had stood beside the litter in the square, and had watched Kynon with such bleak hatred.

"Well," said Stark. "And what do you want with me, little one?"

She answered, "My name is Fianna. And I do not intend to kill you, neither will I run away."

Stark let his hands drop. "Did you follow me, Fianna?"

"I did. Delgaun's palace is full of hidden ways, and I know them all. I was listening behind the panel in the council room. I heard you speak out against Kynon, and I heard Delgaun's order, just now."

"So?"

"So, if you meant what you said about the tribes, you had better get away now, while you have the chance. Kynon lied to you. He will use you, and then kill you, as he will use and then destroy his own people." Her voice was hot with bitter fury.

Stark gave her a slow smile that might have meant anything, or nothing.

"You're a Valkisian, Fianna. What do you care what happens to the barbarians?"

Her slightly tilted green eyes looked scornfully into his.

"I'm not trying to trap you, Earthman. I hate Kynon. And my mother was a woman of the desert."

She paused, then went on sombrely, "Also, I serve the lady Berild, and I have learned many things. There is trouble coming, greater trouble than Kynon knows." She asked, suddenly, "What do you know of the Ramas?"

"Nothing," he answered, "except that they don't exist now, if they ever did."

Fianna gave him an odd look. "Perhaps they don't. Will you listen to me, Earthman from Mercury? Will you get away, now that you know you're marked for death?"

Stark said, "No."

"Even if I tell you that Delgaun has set a trap for you at Kala's?"

"No. But I will thank you for your warning, Fianna."

He bent and kissed her, because she was very young and honest. Then he turned and went on his way.

V

Night came swiftly. Stark left behind him the torches and the laughter and the sounding harps, coming into the streets of the old city where there was nothing but silence and the light of the low moons.

He saw the lower quays, great looming shapes of marble rounded and worn by time, and went toward them. Presently he found that he was following a faint but definite path, threaded between the ancient houses. It was very still, so that the dry whisper of the drifting dust was audible.

He passed under the shadow of the quays, and turned into a broad way that had once led up from the harbour. A little way ahead, on the other side, he saw a tall building, half fallen in ruin. Its windows were shattered, barred with light, and from it came the sound of voices and a thin thread of music, very reedy and evil.

Stark approached it, slipping through the ragged shadows as though he had no more weight to him than a drift of smoke. Once a door banged and a man came out of Kala's and passed by, going down to Valkis. Stark saw his face in the moonlight. It was the face of a beast, rather than a man. He muttered to himself as he went, and once he laughed, and Stark felt a loathing in him.

He waited until the sound of footsteps had died away. The ruined houses gave no sign of danger. A lizard rustled between the stones, and that was all. The moonlight lay bright and still on Kala's door.

Stark found a little shard of rock and tossed it, so that it make a sharp snicking sound against the shadowed wall beyond him. Then he held his breath, listening.

No one, nothing, stirred. Only the dry wind sighed in the empty houses.

Stark went out, across the open space, and nothing happened. He flung open the door of Kala's dive.

Yellow light spilled out, and a choking wave of hot and stuffy air. Inside, there were tall lamps with quartz lenses, each of which poured down a beam of throbbing, gold-orange light. And in the little pools of radiance, on filthy furs and cushions on the floor, lay men and women whose faces were slack and bestial.

Stark realized now what secret vice Kala sold here. Shanga—the going back—the radiation that caused temporary artificial atavism and let men wallow for a time in beasthood. It was supposed to have been stamped out when the Lady Fand's dark Shanga ring had been destroyed. But it still persisted, in places like this outside the law.

He looked for Freka, and recognized the tall barbarian. He was sprawled under one of the Shanga lamps, eyes closed, face brutish, growling and twitching in sleep like the beast he had temporarily become.

A voice spoke from behind Stark's shoulder. "I am Kala. What do you wish, Outlander?"

He turned. Kala might have been beautiful once, a thousand years ago as you reckon sin. She wore still the sweet chiming bells in her hair, and Stark thought of Fianna. The woman's ravaged face turned him sick. It was like the reedy, piping music, woven out of the very heart of evil.

Yet her eyes were shrewd, and he knew that she had not missed his searching look around the room, nor his interest in Freka. There was a note of warning in her voice.

He did not want trouble, yet. Not until he found some hint of the trap Fianna had told him of.

He said, "Bring me wine."

Will you try the lamp of Going-back, Outlander? It brings much joy."

"Perhaps later. Now, I wish wine."

She went away, clapping her hands for a slatternly wench who came between the sprawled figures with an earthern mug. Stark sat down beside a table, where his back was to the wall and he could see both the door and the whole room.

Kala had returned to her own heap of furs by the door, but her basilisk eyes were alert.

Stark made a pretense of drinking, but his mind was very busy, very cold.

Perhaps this, in itself, was the trap. Freka was temporarily a beast. He would fight, and Kala would shriek, and the other dull-eyed brutes would rise and fight also.

But he would have needed no warning about that—and Delgaun himself had said there would be trouble.

No. There was something more.

He let his gaze wander over the room. It was large, and there were other rooms off it, the openings hung with ragged curtains. Through the rents, Stark could see others of Kala's customers sprawled under Shanga-lamps, and some of these had gone so far back from human-ity that they were hideous to behold. But still there was no sign of danger to himself.

There was only one odd thing. The room nearest to where Freka sat was empty, and its curtains were only partly drawn.

Stark began to brood on the emptiness of that room.

He beckoned Kala to him. "I will try the lamp," he said. "But I wish privacy. Have it brought to that room, there."

Kala said, "That room is taken."

"But I see no one!"

"It is taken, it is paid for, and no one may enter. I will have your lamp brought here."

"No," said Stark. "The hell with it. I'm going."

He flung down a coin and went out. Moving swiftly outside, he placed his eye to a crack in the nearest shutter, and waited.

Luhar of Venus came out of the empty room. His face was worried, and Stark smiled. He went back and stood flat against the wall beside the door.

In a moment it opened and the Venusian came out, drawing his gun as he did so.

Stark jumped him.

Luhar let out one angry cry. His gun went off a vicious streak of flame across the moonlight, and then Stark's great hand crushed the bones of his wrist together so that he dropped it clashing on the stones. He whirled around, raking Stark's face with his nails as he clawed for the Earthman's eyes, and Stark hit him. Luhar fell, rolling over, and before he could scramble up again Stark had picked up the gun and thrown it away into the ruins across the street.

Luhar came up from the pavement in one catlike spring. Stark fell with him, back through Kala's door, and they rolled together among the foul furs and cushions. Luhar was built of spring steel, with no softness in him anywhere, and his long fingers were locked around Stark's throat.

Kala screamed with fury. She caught a whip from among her cushions—a traditional weapon along the Low Canals—and began to lash the two men impartially, her hair flying in tangled locks across her face. The bestial figures under the lamps shambled to their feet, and growled.

The long lash ripped Stark's shirt and the flesh of his back beneath it. He snarled and staggered to his feet, with Luhar still clinging to the death grip on his throat. He pushed Luhar's face way from him with both hands and threw himself forward, over a table, so that Luhar was crushed beneath him.

The Venusian's breath left him with a whistling grunt. His lingers relaxed. Stark struck his hands away. He rose and bent over Luhar and picked him up, gripping him cruelly so that he turned white with the pain, and raised him high and flung him bodily into the growling, beast-faced men who were shambling toward him.

Kala leaped at Stark, cursing, striking him with the coiling lash. He turned. The thin veneer of civilisation was gone from Stark now, erased in a second by the first hint of battle. His eyes blazed with a cold light. He took the whip out of Kala's hand and laid his palm across her evil face, and she fell and lay still.

He faced the ring of bestial, Shanga-sodden men who walled him off from what he had been sent to do. There was a reddish tinge to his vision, partly blood, partly sheer rage. He could see Freka standing erect in the corner, his head weaving from side to side brutishly.

Stark raised the whip and strode into the ring of men who were no longer quite men.

Hands struck and clawed him. Bodies reeled and fell away. Blank eyes glittered, and red mouths squealed, and there was a mingling of snarls and bestial laughter in his ears. The blood-lust had spread to these creatures now. They swarmed upon Stark and bore him down with the weight of their writhing bodies.

They bit him and savaged him in a blind way, and he fought his way up again, shaking them off with his great shoulders, trampling them under his boots. The lash hissed and sang, and the smell of blood rose on the choking air.

Freka's dazed, brutish face swam before Stark. The Martian growled and flung himself forward. Stark swung the loaded butt of the whip. It cracked solidly on the Shunni's temple, and he sagged into Stark's arms.

Out of the corner of his eyes, Stark saw Luhar. He had risen and crept around the edge of the fight. He was behind Stark now, and there was a knife in his hand.

Hampered by Freka's weight, Stark could not leap aside. As Luhar rushed in, he crouched and went backward, his head and shoulders taking the Venusian low in the belly. He felt the hot kiss of the blade in his flesh, but the wound was glancing, and before Luhar could strike again, Stark twisted like a great cat and struck down.

Luhar's skull rang on the flagging. The Earthman's fist rose and fell twice. After that, Luhar did not move.

Stark got to his feet. He stood with his knees bent and his shoulders flexed, looking from side to side, and the sound that came out of his throat was one of pure savagery.

He moved forward a step or two, half naked, bleeding, towering like a dark colossus over the lean Martians, and the brutish throng gave back from him. They had taken more mauling than they liked, and there was something about the Outlander's simple desire to rend them apart that penetrated even their Shanga-clouded minds.

Kala sat up on the floor, and snarled, "Get out."

Stark stood a moment or two longer, looking at them. Then he lifted Freka to his feet and laid him over his shoulder like a sack of meal and went out, moving neither fast nor slow, but in a straight line, and way was made for him.

He carried the Shunni down through the silent streets, and into the twisting, crowded ways of Valkis. There, too, the people stared at him and drew back, out of his path. He came to Delgaun's palace. The guards closed in behind him, but they did not ask that he stop.

Delgaun was in the council room, and Berild was still with him. It seemed that they had been waiting, over their wine and their private talk. Delgaun rose to his feet as Stark came in, so sharply that his goblet fell and spilled a red pool of wine at his feet.

Stark let the Shunni drop to the floor.

"I have brought Freka," he said. "Luhar is still at Kala's."

He looked into Delgaun's eyes, golden and cruel, the eyes of her, dream. It was hard not to kill.

Suddenly the woman laughed, very clear and ringing, and her laughter was all for Delgaun.

"Well done, wild man," she said to Stark. "Kynon is lucky to have such a captain. One word for the future, though—watch out for Freka. He won't forgive you this."

Stark said thickly, looking at Delgaun, "This hasn't been a night for forgiveness." Then he added, "I can handle Freka."

Berild said, "I like you, wild man." Her eyes dwelt on Stark's face, curious, compelling. "Ride beside me when we go. I would know more about you."

And she smiled.

A dark flush crept over Delgaun's face. In a voice tight with I fury he said, "Perhaps you've forgotten something, Berild. There is nothing for you in this barbarian, this creature of an hour!"

He would have said more in his anger, but Berild said sharply,

"We will not speak of time. Go now, Stark. Be ready at midnight."

Stark went. And as he went, his brow was furrowed deep by a strange doubt.

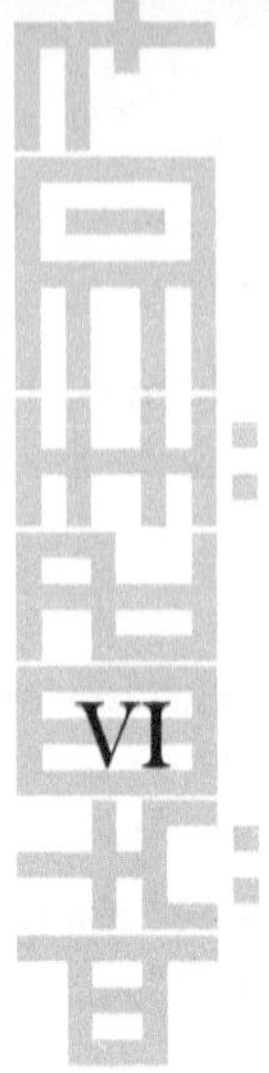

VI

At midnight, in the great square of the slave market, Kynon's caravan formed again and went out of Valkis with thundering drums and skirling pipes. Delgaun was there to see them go, and the cheering of the people rang after them on the desert wind.

Stark rode alone. He was in a brooding mood and wanted no company, least of all that of the Lady Berild. She was beautiful, she was dangerous, and she belonged to Kynon, or to Delgaun, or perhaps to both of them. In Stark's experience, women like that were sudden death, and he wanted no part of her. At any rate, not yet.

Luhar rode ahead with Kynon. He had come dragging into the square at the mounting, his face battered and swollen, an ugly look in his eyes. Kynon gave one quick look from him to Stark, who had his own scars, and said harshly,

"Delgaun tells me there's a blood feud between you two. I want no more of it, understand? After you're paid off you can kill each other and welcome, but not until then. Is that clear?"

Stark nodded, keeping his mouth shut. Luhar muttered assent, and they had not looked at each other since.

Freka rode in his customary place by Kynon, which put him near to Luhar. It seemed to Stark that their beasts swung close together more often than was necessary from the roughness of the track.

The big barbarian captain sat rigidly erect in his saddle, but Stark had seen his face in the torchlight, sick and sweating, with the brute look still clouding his eyes. There was a purple mark on his temple, but Stark was quite sure that Berild had spoken the truth—Freka would not forgive him either the indignity or the hangover of his unfinished wallow under the lamps of Shanga.

The dead sea bottom widened away under the black sky. As they left the lights of Valkis behind, winding their way over the sand and the ribs of coral, dropping lower with every mile into the vast basin, it was hard to believe that there could be life anywhere on a world that could produce such cosmic desolation.

The little moons fled away, trailing their eerie shadows over rock formations tortured into impossible shapes by wind and water, peering into clefts that seemed to have no bottom, turning the sand white as bone. The iron stars blazed, so close that the wind seemed edged with their frosty light. And in all that endless space nothing moved, and the silence was so deep that the coughing howl of a sand-cat far away to the east made Stark jump with its loudness.

Yet Stark was not oppressed by the wilderness. Born and bred to the wild and barren places, this desert was more kin to him than the cities of men.

After a while there was a jangling of brazen bangles behind and Fianna came up. He smiled at her, and she said rather sullenly, "The Lady Berild sent me, to remind you of her wish."

Stark glanced to where the scarlet-curtained litter rocked mg, and his eyes glinted.

"She's not one to let go of a thing, is she?"

"No." Fianna saw that no one was within earshot, and then said quietly, "Was it as I said, at Kala's?"

Stark nodded. "I think, little one, that I owe you my life. Luhar would have killed me as soon as I tackled Freka."

He reached over and touched her hand where it lay on the bridle. She smiled, a young girl's smile that seemed very sweet in the moonlight, honest and comradely.

It was odd to be talking of death with a pretty girl in the moonlight.

Stark said, "Why does Delgaun want to kill me?"

"He gave no reason, when he spoke to the man from Venus. But perhaps I can guess. He knows that you're as strong as he is, and so he fears you. Also, the Lady Berild looked at you in a certain way."

"I thought Berild was Kynon's woman."

"Perhaps she is—for the time," answered Fianna enigmatically. Then she shook her head, glancing around with what was almost fear. "I have risked much already. Please—don't let it be known that I've spoken to you, beyond what I was sent to say."

Her eyes pleaded with him, and Stark realised with a shock that Fianna, too, stood on the edge of a quicksand.

"Don't be afraid," he said, and meant it. "We'd better go."

She swung her beast around, and as she did so she whispered, "Be careful, Eric John Stark!"

Stark nodded. He rode behind her, thinking that he liked the sound of his name on her lips.

The Lady Berild lay among her furs and cushions, and even then there was no indolence about her. She was relaxed as a cat is, perfectly at ease and yet vibrant with life. In the shadows of the litter her skin showed silver-white and her loosened hair was a sweet darkness.

"Are you stubborn, wild man?" she asked. "Or do you find me distasteful?"

He had not realised before how rich and soft her voice was. He looked down at the magnificent supple length of her, and said,

"I find you most damnably attractive—and that's why I'm stubborn."

"Afraid?"

"I'm taking Kynon's pay. Should I take his woman also?"

She laughed, half scornfully. "Kynon's ambitions leave no room for me. We have an agreement, because a king must have a queen—and he finds my counsel useful. You see, I am ambitious, too! Apart from that, there is nothing."

Stark looked at her, trying to read her smoke-grey eyes in the gloom. "And Delgaun?"

"He wants me, but …" She hesitated, and then went on, in a tone quite different from before, her voice low and throbbing with a secret pleasure as vast and elemental as the star-shot sky.

"I belong to no one," she said. "I am my own."

Stark knew that for the moment she had forgotten him.

He rode for a time in silence, and then he said slowly, repeating Delgaun's words,

"Perhaps you have forgotten something, Berild. There is nothing for you in me, the creature of an hour."

He saw her start, and for a moment her eyes blazed and her breath was sharply drawn. Then she laughed, and said,

"The wild man is also a parrot. And an hour can be a long time— as long as eternity, if one wills it so."

"Yes," said Stark, "I have often thought so, waiting for death to come at me out of a crevice in the rocks. The great lizard stings, and his bite is fatal."

He leaned over in the saddle, his shoulders looming above hers, naked in the biting wind.

"My hours with women are short ones," he said. "They come after the battle, when there is time for such things. Perhaps then I'll come and see you."

He spurred away and left her without a backward look, and the skin of his back tingled with the expectancy of a flying knife.

But the only thing that followed him was a disturbing echo of laughter down the wind.

Dawn came. Kynon beckoned Stark to his side, and pointed out at the cruel waste of sand, with here and there a reef of basalt black against the burning white.

"This is the country you will lead your men over. Learn it." He was speaking to Luhar as well. "Learn every water hole, every vantage point, every trail that leads toward the Border. There are no better fighters than the Dryland men when they're well led, and you must prove to them that you can lead. You'll work with their own chief-tains—Freka, and the others you'll meet when we reach Sinharat."

Luhar said, "Sinharat?"

"My headquarters. It's about seven days" march—an island city, old as the moons. The Rama cult was strong there, legend has it, and it's a sort of holy place to the tribesmen. That's why I picked it."

He took a deep breath and smiled, looking out over the dead sea bottom toward the Border, and his eyes held the same pitiless light as the sun that baked the desert.

"Very soon, now," he said, more to himself than the others. "Only a handful of days before we drown the Border states in their own blood. And after that …"

He laughed, very softly, and said no more. Stark could believe that what Berild said of him was true. There was a flame of ambition in Kynon that would let nothing stand in its way.

He measured the size and the strength of the tall barbarian, the eagle look of his face and the iron that lay beneath his joviality. Then Stark, too, stared off toward the Border and wondered if he would ever see Tarak or hear Simon Ashton's voice again.

For three days they marched without incident. At noon they made a dry camp and slept away the blazing hours, and then went on again under a darkening sky, a long line of tall men and rangy beasts, with the scarlet litter blooming like a strange flower in the midst of it. Jingling bridles and dust, and padded hoofs trampling the bones of the sea, toward the island city of Sinharat.

Stark did not speak again to Berild, nor did she send for him.

Fianna would pass him in the camp, and smile sidelong, and go on. For her sake, he did not stop her.

Neither Luhar nor Freka came near him. They avoided him pointedly, except when Kynon called them all together to discuss some point of strategy. But the two seemed to have become friends, and drank together from the same bottle of wine.

Stark slept always beside his mount, his back guarded and his gun loose. The hard lessons learned in his childhood had stayed with him, and if there was a footfall near him in the dust he woke often before the beast did.

Toward morning of the fourth night the wind, that never seemed to falter from its steady blowing, began to drop. At dawn it was dead still, and the rising sun had a tinge of blood. The dust rose under the feet of the beasts and fell again where it had risen.

Stark began to sniff the air. More and more often he looked toward the north, where there was a long slope as flat as his palm that stretched away farther than he could see.

A restless unease grew within him. Presently he spurred ahead to join Kynon.

"There is a storm coming," he said, and turned his head northward again.

Kynon looked at him curiously.

"You even have the right direction," he said. "One might think you were a native." He, too, gazed with brooding anger at the long sweep of emptiness.

"I wish we were closer to the city. But one place is as bad as another when the khamsin blows, and the only thing to do is keep moving. You're a dead dog if you stop—dead and buried."

He swore, with a curious admixture of blunt Anglo-Saxon in his Martian profanity, as though the storm were a personal enemy.

"Pass the word along to force it—dump whatever they have to to lighten the loads. And get Berild out of that damned litter. Stick by her, will you, Stark? I've got to stay here, at the head of the line. And don't get separated. Above all, don't get separated!"

Stark nodded and dropped back. He got Berild mounted, and they left the litter there, a bright patch of crimson on the sand, its curtains limp in the utter stillness.

Nobody talked much. The beasts were urged on to the top of heir speed. They were nervous and fidgety, inclined to break nit of line and run for it. The sun rose higher.

One hour.

The windless air shimmered. The silence lay upon the caravan with a crushing hand. Stark went up and down the line, lending a hand to the sweating drovers with the pack animals that now carried only water skins and a bare supply of food. Fianna rode close beside Berild.

Two hours.

For the first time that day there was a sound in the desert.

It came from far off, a moaning wail like the cry of a giantess in travail. It rushed closer, rising as it did so to a dry and bitter shriek that filled the whole sky, shook it, and tore it open, letting in all the winds of hell.

It struck swiftly. One moment the air was clear and motionless. The next, it was blind with dust and screaming as it fled, tearing with demoniac fury at everything in its path.

Stark spurred toward the women, who were only a few feet away but already hidden by the veil of mingled dust and sand. Someone blundered into him in the murk. Long hair whipped across his face and he reached out, crying "Fianna! Fianna!" A woman's hand caught his, and a voice answered, but he could not hear the words.

Then, suddenly, his beast was crowded by other scaly bodies. The woman's grip had broken. Hard masculine hands clawed at him. He could make out, dimly, the features of two men, close to his.

Luhar, and Freka.

His beast gave a great lurch, and sprang forward. Stark was dragged from the saddle, to fall backward into the raging sand.

VII

He lay half-stunned for a moment, his breath knocked out of him. There was a terrible reptilian screaming sounding thin through the roar of the wind. Vague shapes bolted past him, and twice he was nearly crushed by their trampling hooves.

Luhar and Freka must have waited their chance. It was so beautifully easy. Leave Stark alone and afoot, and the storm and the desert between them would do the work, with no blame attaching to any man.

Stark got to his feet, and a human body struck him at the knees so that he went down again. He grappled with it, snarling, before he realised that the flesh between his hands was soft and draped in silken cloth. Then he saw that he was holding Berild.

"It was I," she gasped, "and not Fianna."

Her words reached him very faintly, though he knew she was yelling at the top of her lungs. She must have been knocked from her own mount when Luhar thrust between them.

Gripping her tightly, so that she should not be blown away, Stark struggled up again. With all his strength, it was almost impossible to stand.

Blinded, deafened, half strangled, he fought his way forward a few paces, and suddenly one of the pack beasts loomed shadow-like beside him, going by with a rush and a squeal.

By the grace of Providence and his own swift reflexes, he caught its pack lashings, clinging with the tenacity of a man determined not to die. It floundered about, dragging them, until Berild managed to grasp its trailing halter rope. Between them, they fought the creature down.

Stark clung to its head while the woman clambered to its back, twisting her arm through the straps of the pad. A silken scarf whipped toward him. He took it and tied it over the head of the beast so it could breathe, and after that it was quieter.

There was no direction, no sight of anything, in that howling inferno. The caravan seemed to have been scattered like a drift of autumn leaves. Already, in the few brief moments he had stood still, Stark's legs were buried to the knees in a substratum of sand that rolled like water. He pulled himself free and started on, going nowhere, remembering Kynon's words.

Berild ripped her thin robe apart and gave him another strip of silk for himself. He bound it over his nose and eyes, and some of the choking and the blindness abated.

Stumbling, staggering, beaten by the wind as a child is beaten by a strong man, Stark went on, hoping desperately to find the main body of the caravan, and knowing somehow that the hope was futile.

The hours that followed were nightmare. He shut his mind to them, in a way that a civilised man would have found impossible. In his childhood there had been days, and nights, and the problems had been simple ones—how to survive one span of light that one might then struggle to survive the span of darkness that came after. One thing, one danger, at a time.

Now there was a single necessity. Keep moving. Forget tomorrow, or what happened to the caravan, or where the little Fianna with her bright eyes may be. Forget thirst, and the pain of breathing, and the fiery lash of sand on naked skin. Only don't stand still.

It was growing dark when the beast fell against a half-buried boulder and snapped its foreleg. Stark gave it a quick and merciful death. They took the straps from the pad and linked themselves together. Each took as much food as they could carry, and Stark shouldered the single skin of water that fortune had vouchsafed them.

They staggered on, and Berild did not whimper.

Night came, and still the khamsin blew. Stark wondered at the woman's strength, for he had to help her only when she fell. He had lost all feeling himself. His body was merely a thing that continued to move only because it had been ordered not to stop.

The haze in his own mind had grown as thick as the black obscurity of the night. Berild had ridden all day, but he had walked, and there was an end even to his strength. He was approaching it now, and was too weary even to be afraid.

He became aware at some indeterminate time that Berild had fallen and was dragging her weight against the straps. He turned blindly to help her up. She was saying something, crying his name, striking at him so that he should hear her words and understand.

At last he did. He pulled the wrappings from his face and breathed clean air. The wind had fallen. The sky was growing clear.

He dropped in his tracks and slept, with the exhausted woman half dead beside him.

Thirst brought them both awake in the early dawn. They drank from the skin, and then sat for a time looking at the desert, and at each other, thinking of what lay ahead.

"Do you know where we are?" Stark asked.

"Not exactly." Berild's face was shadowed with weariness. It had changed, and somehow, to Stark, it had grown more beautiful, because there was no weakness in it.

She thought a minute, looking at the sun. "The wind blew from the north," she said. "Therefore we have come south from the track. Sinharat lies that way, across the waste they call the Belly of Stones." She pointed to the north and east.

"How far?"

"Seven, eight days, afoot."

Stark measured their supply of water and shook his head. "It'll be dry walking."

He rose and took up the skin, and Berild came beside him without a word. Her red hair hung loose over her shoulders. The rags of her silken robe had been torn away by the wind, leaving her only the loose skirt of the desert women, and her belt and collar of jewels.

She walked erect with a steady, swinging stride, and it was almost impossible for Stark to remember her as she had been, riding like a lazy queen in her scarlet litter.

There was no way to shelter themselves from the midday sun. The sun of Mars at its worst, however, was only a pale candle beside the sun of Mercury, and it did not bother Stark. He made Berild lie in the shadow of his own body, and he watched her face, relaxed and unfamiliar in sleep.

For the first time, then, he was conscious of a strangeness in her. He had seen so little of her before, in Valkis, and almost nothing on the trail. Now, there was little of her mind or heart that she could conceal from him.

Or was there? There were moments, while she slept, when hr shadows of strange dreams crossed her face. Sometimes, in t he unguarded moment of waking, he would see in her eyes a Iook he could not read, and his primitive senses quivered with a vague ripple of warning.

Yet all through those blazing days and frosty nights, tortured with thirst and weary to exhaustion, Berild was magnificent. Her white skin was darkened by the sun and her hair became a wild red mane, but she smiled and set her feet resolutely by his, and Stark thought she was the most beautiful creature he had ever seen.

On the fourth day they climbed a scarp of limestone worn in ages past by the sea, and looked out over the place called the Belly of Stones.

The sea-bottom curved downward below them into a sort of gigantic basin, the farther rim of which was lost in shimmering waves of heat. Stark thought that never, even on Mercury, had he seen a place more cruel and utterly forsaken of gods or men.

It seemed as though some primal glacier must have met its death here in the dim dawn of Mars, hollowing out its own grave. The body of the glacier had melted away, but its bones were left.

Bones of basalt, of granite and marble and porphyry, of every conceivable colour and shape and size, picked up by the ice as it marched southward from the pole and dropped here as a cairn to mark its passing.

The Belly of Stones. Stark thought that its other name was Death.

For the first time, Berild faltered. She sat down and bent her head over her hands.

"I am tired," she said. "Also, I am afraid."

Stark asked, "Has it ever been crossed?"

"Once. But they were a war party, mounted and well supplied."

Stark looked out across the stones. "We will cross it," he said.

Berild raised her head. "Somehow I believe you." She rose slowly and put her hands on his breast, over the strong beating of his heart.

"Give me your strength, wild man," she whispered. "I shall need it."

He drew her to him and kissed her, and it was a strange and painful kiss, for their lips were cracked and bleeding from their terrible thirst. Then they went down together into the place called the Belly of Stones.

VIII

THE DESERT HAD BEEN A PLEASANT AND KINDLY PLACE. STARK looked back upon it with longing. And yet this inferno of blazing rock was so like the valleys of his boyhood that it did not occur to him to lie down and die.

They rested for a time in the sheltered crevice under a great leaning slab of blood-red stone, moistening their swollen tongues with a few drops of stinking water from the skin. At nightfall they drank the last of it, but Berild would not let him throw the skin away.

Darkness, and a lunar silence. The chill air sucked the day's heat out of the rocks and the iron frost came down, so that Stark and the red-haired woman must keep moving or freeze.

Stark's mind grew clouded. He spoke from time to time, in a croaking whisper, dropping back into the harsh mother-tongue of the Twilight Belt. It seemed to him that he was hunting, as he had so many times before, in the waterless places—for the blood of the great lizard would save him from thirst.

But nothing lived in the Belly of Stones. Nothing, but the two who crept and staggered across it under the low moons.

Berild fell, and could not rise again. Stark crouched beside her. Her face stared up at him, while in the moonlight, her eyes burning and strange.

I will not die!" she whispered, not to him, but to the gods. "I will not die!"

And she clawed the sand and the bitter rocks, dragging herself onward It was uncanny, the madness that she had for life.

Stark raised her up and carried her. His breath came in deep

sobbing gasps. After a while he, too, fell. He went on like a beast fours, dragging the woman.

I He knew dimly that he was climbing. There was a glimmering of dawn in the sky. His hands slipped on a lip of sand and he went rolling down a smooth slope. At length he stopped and lay in his back like a dead thing.

The sun was high when consciousness returned to him. He saw Berild lying near him and crawled to her, shaking her until her eyes opened. Her hands moved feebly and her lips formed the same four words. I will not die.

Stark strained his eyes to the horizon, praying for a glimpse of Sinharat, but there was nothing, only emptiness and sand. With great difficulty he got the woman to her feet, supporting her.

He tried to tell her that they must go on, but he could no longer form the words. He could only gesture and urge her forward, in the direction of the city.

But she refused to go. "Too far … die … without water …" He knew that she was right, but still he was not ready to give up.

She began to move away from him, toward the south, and he thought that she had gone mad and was wandering. Then he saw that she was peering with awful intensity at the line of the scarp that formed this wall of the Belly of Stones. It rose into a great ridge, serrated like the backbone of a whale, and some three miles away a long dorsal fin of reddish rock curved out into the desert.

Berild made a little sobbing noise in her throat. She began to plod toward the distant promontory.

Stark caught up with her. He tried to stop her, but she would not be stopped, turning a feral glare upon him.

She croaked, "Water!" and pointed.

He was sure now that she was mad. He told her so, forcing the painful words out of his throat, reminding her of Sinharat and that she was going away from any possible help.

She said again, quite sanely, "Too far. Two—three days without water," She pointed. "Monastery—old well—a chance …"

Stark decided that he had little to lose by trusting her. He nodded and went with her toward the curve of rock.

The three miles might have been three hundred. At last they came up under the ragged cliffs—and there was nothing there but sand.

Stark looked at the woman. A great rage and a deep sense of futility came over him. They were indeed lost.

But Berild had gone a few steps farther. With a hoarse cry, she bent over what had seemed merely a slab of stone fallen from the cliff, and Stark saw that it was a carven pillar, half buried. Now he was able to make out the mounded shape of a ruin, of which only the foundations and a few broken columns were left.

For a long while Berild stood by the pillar, her eyes closed. Stark got the uncanny feeling that she was visualizing the place as it had been, though the wall must have been dust a thousand years ago. Presently she moved. He followed her, and it was strange to see her, on the naked sand, treading the arbitrary patterns of vanished corridors.

She came to a halt, in a broad flat space that might once have been a central courtyard. There she fell on her knees and began to dig.

Stark got down beside her. They scrabbled like a pair of dogs in the yielding sand. Stark's nails slipped across something hard, and there was a yellow glint through the dusty ochre. Within a few minutes they had bared a golden cover six feet across, very massive and wonderfully carved with the symbols of some lost god of the sea.

Stark struggled to lift the thing away. He could not move it. Then Berild pressed a hidden spring and the cover slid back of itself. Beneath it, sweet and cold, protected through all these ages, water stirred gently against mossy stones.

An hour later, Stark and Berild lay sleeping soaked to the skin, their very hair dripping with the blessed dampness.

That night, when the low moons roved over the desert, by the well, drowsy with an animal sense of rest and repletion.And Stark looked at the woman and said, "I know you now."

"What do you know, wild man?"

Stark said quietly, "You are a Rama."

She did not answer at once. Then she said, "I was bred in these these deserts. Is it so strange that I should know of this well?"

"Strange that you didn't mention it before. You were afraid, weren't you, that if you led me here your secret would come out? But it was that, or die."

He leaned forward, studying her.'If you had led me straight to the well, I might not have wondered. But you had to stop and remember, how the halls were built and where the doorways were that led to the inner court. You lived in this place when it was whole. And no one, not even Kynon himself, knows of it but you."

"You dream, wild man. The moon is in your eyes."

Stark shook his head slowly. "I know."

She laughed, and stretched her arms wide on the sand.

"But I am young," she said. "And men have told me I am beautiful. It is good to be young, for youth has nothing to do with ashes and empty skulls."

She touched his arm, and little darts of fire went through his flesh, warm from his fingertips.

"Forget your dreams, wild man. They're madness, gone with the morning."

He looked down at her in the clear pale light, and she was young, and beautifully made, and her lips were smiling.

He bent his head. Her arms went round him. Her hair blew soft against his cheek. Then, suddenly, she set her teeth cruelly into his lip. He cried out and thrust her away, and she sat back on her heels, mocking him.

"That," she said, "is because you called Fianna's name instead of mine, when the storm broke."

Stark cursed her. There was a taste of blood in his mouth. He reached out and caught her, and again she laughed, a peculiarly sweet, wicked sound.

The wind blew over them, sighing, and the desert was very still.

For two days they remained among the ruins. At evening of the second day Stark filled the water skin, and Berild replaced the golden cover on the well. They began the last long march toward Sinharat.

IX

Stark saw it rising against the morning sky—a city of gold and marble, high on an island of rose-red coral laid bare by the vanished sea. Sinharat, the Ever Living.

Yet it had died. As he came closer to it, plodding slowly through the sand, he saw that the place was no more than a beautiful corpse, the lovely towers broken, the roofless palaces open to the sky. Whatever life Kynon and his armies might have foisted upon Sinharat was no more than the fleeting passage of ants across the perfect bones of the dead.

"What was it like before?" he asked, "with the blue water around it, and the banners flying?"

Berild turned a dark, calculating look upon him.

"I told you before to forget that madness. If you talk it, no one will believe you."

"No one?"

"You had best not anger me, wild man," she said quietly. "I may be your only hope of life, before this is over."

They did not speak again, going with slow weary steps toward the city.

In the desert below the coral cliffs the armies of Kynon were encamped. The tall warriors of Kesh and Shun waiting, with their women and their beasts and their shining spears, for the pipers to cry them over the Border. The skin tents and the long picket lines were too many to count. In the distance, a convertible Kallman spacer that Stark recognised as Knighton's made an ugly, jarring incongruity.

Lookouts sighted the two toiling figures in the distance. Men and women and children began to stream out across the sand, and presently a great cheering arose. Where he had looked on emptiness for days, Stark was smothered now by the press of thousands. Berild was picked up and carried on the shoulders of two chiefs, and men would have carried Stark also, but he fought diem off.

Broad flights of steps were cut in the coral. The throng flowed upward along them. Ahead of them all went Eric John Stark, and Hie was smiling. From time to time he asked a question, and men drew back from that question, and his smile.

Up the steps and into the streets of Sinharat he went, with a slow, restless stride, asking,

"Where is Luhar of Venus?"

Every man there read death in his face, but they did not try to stop him.

People came out of the graceful ruins, drawn by the clamour, and the tide rolled down the broad ways, the rose-red streets of coral, until it spread out in the square before a great palace of gold and ivory and white marble blinding in the sun.

Luhar of Venus came down the terraced steps, fresh from sleep, his pale hair tumbled, his eyes still drowsy.

Others came through the door behind him. Stark did not see them. They did not matter. Berild didn't matter, calling his name from where she sat on the shoulders of the chiefs. Nothing, no one mattered, but himself and Luhar.

He crossed the square, not hurrying, a dark ravaged giant in rags. He saw Luhar pause on the bottom step. He saw the sleep and the vagueness go out of the Venusian's eyes as they rested first on the red-haired woman, then on himself. He saw the fear come into them, and the undying hate.

Someone got between him and Luhar. Stark lifted the man and flung him aside without breaking his stride, and went on. Luhar half turned. He would have run away, back into the palace, but there were too many now between him and the door. He crouched and drew his gun.

Stark sprang.

He came like a great black panther leaping, and he struck low. Luhar's shot went over his back. After that there was no more shooting. There was a moment, terribly short and silent, in which the two men lay entangled, straining against each other in a sort of stasis. Then Luhar screamed.

Stark knew dimly that there were hands, many of them, trying to drag him away. He clung growling to the Venusian until he was torn loose by main force. He struggled against his captors, and through a red haze he saw Kynon's face, close to his and very angry. Luhar was not yet dead.

"I warned you, Stark!" said Kynon furiously. "I warned you."

Men were bending over Luhar. Knighton, Walsh, Themis, Arrod. Stark saw that Delgaun was among them. He did not question at the time how word had gone back to Valkis and sent Delgaun racing across the dead sea bottom with his hired bravos to search for the red-haired woman. It was right that Delgaun should be there.

In short ragged sentences, Stark told how Luhar and Freka had tried to kill him, and how Berild had been lost with him.

Kynon turned to the Venusian. Death was already glazing the cloud-grey eyes, but it had not quenched the hatred and venom.

"He lies," whispered Luhar. "I saw him—he tried to run away and take the woman with him."

Luhar of Venus, taking vengeance with his last breath.

Freka pushed forward, transparently eager to pick up his cue. "It is so," he said. "I was with Luhar. I saw it also."

Delgaun laughed. Cruel, silent laughter. He stood up, and looked at Berild.

Berild's eyes were blazing. She ignored Delgaun and spoke to Kynon.

"You fool. Can't you see that they hate him? What Stark says is true. And I would have died in the desert because of them, if Stark hadn't been a better man than all of you."

"Strange words," said Delgaun, "coming from a man's own mate. Perhaps Luhar did lie, after all. Perhaps it was not Stark who tried to run away, but you."

She cursed him, with an ancient curse, and Kynon looked at her, sullenly. He said to the men who held Stark, "Chain him below, in the dungeons." Then he took Berild's arm and went with her into the palace.

Stark fought until someone behind him knocked him on the head with the butt of a spear. The last thing he saw was the face of Fianna, standing out from the crowd, wide-eyed with pity and love.

He came to in a place of cold, dry stone. There was an iron collar around his neck, and a five-foot chain ran from it to a ring in the wall. The cell was small. A gate of iron bars closed the entrance. Beyond was an open well, with other cell doors around it, and above were thick stone gratings open to the sky. He guessed that the place was built beneath some inner court of he palace.

There were no other prisoners. But there was a guard, a thick-shouldered barbarian who sat on the execution block in the centre of the well, with a sword and a jug of wine. A guard who watched the captive Stark, and smiled.

Freka.

When he saw that Stark was awake, Freka lifted up the jug and laughed. "Here's to Death," he said. For no one else comes here!"

He drank, and after that he did not speak, only sat and smiled.

Stark said nothing either. He waited, with the same unhuman patience he had shown when he waited for his captors under the tor.

The dim daylight faded from the gratings. Darkness came, and the pale glimmer of the moons. Freka became a silvered statue of a man, sitting on the block. Stark's eyes glowed.

The empty jug dropped and broke. Freka rose. He took the naked sword in his hand and crossed the open space to the cell. He lifted the outer bar away. It fell with a great echoing clang, and Freka entered.

"Stand up, Outlander," he said. "Stand up and face the steel. After that you'll sleep in a coral pit, and not even the worms will find you."

"Beast of Shanga!" Stark said contemptuously, and set his back against the wall, to give himself all the slack of the chain.

He saw the bright steel glimmer in the air, up and down again, but when the blow fell he had leaped aside, and the point struck ringing against the stone. Stark darted in to grapple.

His fingers slipped on hard muscle, and Freka wrenched away. He was a fighting man, and no weakling. The iron collar dug painfully into the Earthman's throat and the heavy chain threw him backward. Freka laughed, deep in his chest. The sword glinted hungrily.

Then, as though she had taken shape suddenly from the shadows, Fianna was in the doorway. The little gun in her hand made a hissing spurt of flame. Freka screamed once, and fell. He did not move again.

"The swine," Fianna said, without emotion. "Delgaun ordered him to wait, until it was sure that Kynon would not come down to talk to you. Then the story was to be that you had escaped somehow, with Berild's aid."

She stepped over the body and unlocked the iron collar with a key she took from her girdle.

Stark took her slender shoulders gently between his hands. "Are you a witch-girl, that you know all things and always come when I need you?"

She gave him a deep, strange look. In the dusk, her proud young face was unfamiliar, touched with something fey and sad. He wished that he could see her eyes more clearly.

"I know all things because I must," she told him wearily. "And I think that you are my only hope—perhaps the only hope of Mars."

He drew her to him, and kissed her, and stroked her dark head. "You're too young to concern yourself with the destinies of worlds."

He felt her tremble. "The youth of the body is only illusion, when the mind is old."

"And is yours old, little one?"

"Old," she whispered. "As old as Berild's."

He felt her tears warm against his skin, and she was like a child in her arms.

"Then you know about her," said Stark.

He paused. "And Delgaun?"

"Delgaun also."

"I thought so," Stark said. He nodded, scowling at the barred moonlight in the well. "There are things I must know myself but we'd best get out of here. Did Berild send you?"

"Yes—as soon as she could get the key from Kynon. She is waiting for you." She stirred Freka's body with her foot. "Bring that. We'll hide it in the pit he meant for you."

Stark heaved the body over his shoulder and followed the girl through a twisting maze of corridors, some pitch dark, some feebly lighted by the moons. Fianna moved as surely as though she were in the main square at high noon. There was the silence of death in these cold tunnels, and the dry faint smell of eternity.

At length Fianna whispered. "Here. Be careful."

She put out a hand to guide him, but Stark's eyes were like a cat's in the dark. He made out a space where the rock with which the ancient builders had faced these subterranean ways gave place to the original coral.

Ragged black mouths opened in the coral, entrances to some unguessed catacombs beneath. Stark consigned Freka to the nearest pit, and then reluctantly threw his sword in after him.

"You won't need it," Fianna told him, "and besides, it would be recognised. This will be a bitter night enough, without rousing the men of Shun over Freka's death."

Stark listened to the distant sliding echoes from the pit, and shivered. He had so nearly finished there himself. He was glad to follow Fianna away from that place of darkness and silent death.

He stopped her in a place where a bar of moonlight came splashing through a great crack in the tunnel roof.

"Now," he said, "we will talk."

She nodded. "Yes. The time has come for that."

"There are lies everywhere," said Stark. "I am tangled up in lies. You know the truth that is behind this war of Kynon's. Tell me."

"Kynon's truth is simple," she answered, speaking slowly, choosing her words. "He wants land and power, conquest. He will pour out the blood of his people for that, and after that he plans to use the men of the Low-Canals under Delgaun to keep the tribesmen in line. It may be true, as he said, that they would be satisfied with grazing land and water—but they would lose their freedom, and their pride, and I think he has judged them wrongly. I think they would revolt."

She looked up at Stark. "He planned to use your knowledge, and then destroy you if you became troublesome."

"I guessed that. What about the others?"

"The outlanders? Use them, keep them as subordinates, or pay them off. Kill them, if necessary."

Now," said Stark. "What of Delgaun and Berild?"

Fianna said softly. "Their truth, too, is simple. They took Kynon's idea of empire, and stretched it further. It was Delgaun's idea to bring the strangers in. They would use Kynon and the tribes until the victory was won. Then they would do away with Kynon and rule themselves—with the outlanders and their ships and their powerful weapons to oppress Low-Canaler and Drylander alike.

"That way, they could rape a world. More outland vultures would come, drawn by the smell of loot. The Martian men would fight as long as there was the hope of plunder—after that, they would be slaves to hold the empire. Their masters would grow fat on tribute from the City-States and from the men of Earth who have built here, or who wish to build. An evil plan—but profitable."

Stark thought about Knighton and Walsh of Terra, Themis of Mercury, Arrod of Callisto Colony. He thought of others like them, and what they would do, with their talons hooked in the heart of Mars. He thought of Delgaun's yellow eyes.

He thought of Berild, and he was sick with loathing.

Fianna came close to him, speaking in a different tone that had care and anxiety only for him.

"I have told you this, because I know what Berild plans. Tonight - oh, tonight is a black and evil time, and death waits in Sinharat! It is very close to me, I know. And you must follow own heart, Eric John Stark. I cannot tell you more."

He kissed her again, because she was sweet and very brave. Then she led him on through the dark labyrinth, to where Berild was waiting, with her dangerous beauty and all the evil of the ages in her soul.

X

They came out of the darkness so suddenly that Stark blinked in the unaccustomed light of torches set in great silver sconces on the walls.

The floor had been artificially smoothed, but otherwise the crypt was as the eroding action of the sea had shaped it out of the coral reef. It was not large, and it was like a cavern in a fairy tale, walled and roofed with the fantastic wreathing shapes of the rose-red coral. At one end there was a golden coffer set with naming jewels.

Berild was there. Her wonderful hair was dressed and shining, and her body was clothed all in white, her arms and shoulders warm bronze from the kiss of the desert sun.

Kynon was there, also. He stood motionless and silent, and he did not so much as turn his head when Fianna and Stark came in. His eyes were wide open and blank as a blind man's.

"I have been waiting," said Berild, "and the time is short."

She seemed angry and impatient, and Stark said, "Freka is dead. It was necessary to hide his body."

She nodded and turned to the girl. "Go now, Fianna."

Fianna bent her head and went away. She did not look at Stark. It was as though she had no interest in anything that happened.

Stark looked at Kynon, who had not moved or spoken.

"He is safe enough," said Berild, answering Stark's unspoken question. "I drugged his wine so that his mind was opened to mine, and he is my creature as long as I will it."

Hypnosis, Stark thought. His nerves were beginning to do strange things. He wished desperately that he were back in the cell facing Freka's sword, which at least would deal with him openly and without guile or subterfuge.

Berild set her hands on Stark's shoulders, and smiled as she had done that night by the ancient well.

"I offer you three things tonight, wild man," she said. Her eyes challenged him, and the scent of her hair was sweet and maddening.

"Your life—and power—and myself."

Stark let his hands slip lightly down from her shoulders to her waist. "And how will you do this thing?" he asked.

"Easily," she said, and laughed. She was very proud, and sure of her strength, and glad to be alive. "Oh, very easily. You guessed the truth about me—I am of the Twice Born, the Ramas. I hold the secret of the Sending-on of Minds, which this great ox Kynon pretended to have. I can give you life now—and forever. Remember, wild man—forever!"

He bent his dark face to hers, so that their lips touched, and murmured, "Would I have you forever, Berild?"

"Until you tire of me—or I of you." She kissed him, and then added mockingly, "Delgaun has had me for a thousand years, and I am weary of him. So very weary!"

"A thousand years is a long time," said Stark, "and I am not Delgaun."

"No. You're a beast, a savage, a most magnificent cold-eyed animal, and that is why I love you." She touched the muscle of his breast, and then his throat, and added, "It's a pity there will never be another body like this one. We must keep it as long as we can."

"What is your plan?" Stark asked her.

"Simply this. I will place your mind in Kynon's body. You will be Kynon, with all his power. You will be able then to keep Delgaun in check—later, you can destroy him, but not until after the battle is won, for we need the men of Valkis and Jekkara. You can keep your own body safe from him, and at the worst, if by some chance he should succeed in slaying the man he believes to be you, you will still be alive."

"And after the battle," said Stark softly. "What then, Berild?"

"We will rule together." She held his palms against hers. "You have strong hands, wild man. Would you not like to hold a world between them—and me?"

She looked up at him, her eyes suddenly shrewd and probing. Or do you still believe the nonsense you talked to Kynon, about the tribes?"

Stark smiled. "It's easy to have principles when there's no gain involved. No. I am as my name says—a man without a tribe. I have no loyalties. And if I had, would I remember them now?"

He held her, as she had said, between his hands, and they were very strong.

But even then, Berild could warn him.

"Keep faith with me, then! My wisdom is greater than yours, and I have powers you don't dream of. What I give, I can take away."

For answer, Stark silenced her mouth with his own.

When she drew away, she said rather breathlessly, "Let us hurry. The tribes are gathered, and Kynon was to have given the signal for war at dawn. There is much I must teach you between now and then."

She paused with her hand on the lid of the golden coffer. "This is a secret place," she said quietly. "Since before the ocean died, it has been secret. Not even Kynon knew of it. I think only Delgaun and I, the last of the Twice-Born, knew—and now you."

"What about Fianna?"

Berild shrugged. "She is only my servant. To her, this is only a little cavern where I keep my private wealth."

She pressed a series of patterned bosses in intricate sequence, and there was the sharp click of an opening lock. A shiver ran up along Stark's spine. The beast in him longed to run, to be away from this whole business that smelled of evil. But the man in him knelt at Berild's wish, and waited, and did not flinch when the blank-eyed Kynon came like a moving corpse beside him.

Berild raised the golden lid. And there was a great silence.

On the slave block of Valkis, Kynon had brought forth two crowns of shining crystal and a rod of flame. As glass is to diamond, as the pallid moon to the light of the sun, were those things to the reality.

In her two hands Berild held the ancient crowns of the Ramas, the givers of life. Twin circlets of glorious fire, dimming the shallow glare of the torches, putting a nimbus of light around the white-clad woman so that she was like a goddess walking in a cloud of stars. Stark's whole being contracted to a point of icy pain at the beauty and the wonder and the terror of them.

She set one crown on Kynon's head, and even the drugged automaton shivered and sighed at its touch.

Stark's mind veered away from the incredible thing that was about to happen. It spoke words to him, hurried desperate words of sanity, about the electrical patterns of the mind, and the sensitivity of crystals, and conductors, and electro-magnetic impulses. But that was only the top of his brain. At base it was still the brain of N'Chaka that believed in gods and demons and all the sorceries of darkness. Only pride kept him from cowering abjectly at Berild's feet.

She stood above him, a creature of dreams in the unearthly light. She smiled and whispered, "Do not fear,'—and she placed the second crown upon his head.

A strange, shuddering fire swept through him. It was as though some chip of the primal heart of all creation had been set by an unguessed magic into the cells of the crystal. The force that shaped the universe and scattered forth the stars, and set the great suns to spinning. There was something awesome about it, something almost holy.

And yet he was afraid. Most shockingly afraid.

His brain was set free, in some strange fashion. The walls of his skull vanished. His mind floated in a dim vastness. It was like a tiny sun, glowing, spinning, swelling …

Berild lifted a crystal rod from the coffer, a wand of sorcerous fire. And now Stark's thoughts had lost all track of science. A cloud of misty darkness flowed around him, thickened …

A great leaping flare of light, a distant echo of a cry that he did not recognise as his own, and then …

Nothing.

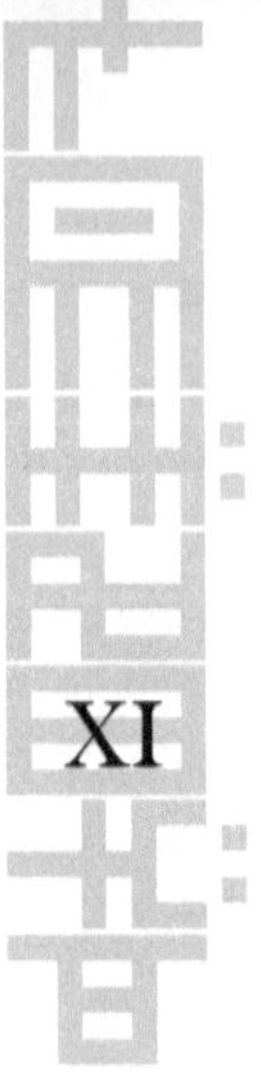

XI

He was lying on his face, his cheek pressed against the cool coral. He opened his eyes, his mind groping for the shreds of some remembered terror. He saw, vaguely at first and then with terrible clarity as his vision became clear, a man lying close beside him.

A tall man, very strongly built, with skin burned almost to blackness by exposure. A man who looked at him with eyes that were startlingly light in his dark face …

His own eyes. His own face. He cried out and struggled to his feet, trembling, staggering, and his body felt strange to him. He looked down upon the strangeness of another man's limbs, the alien shaping of flesh and sinew upon alien bones.

The face of the dark giant who lay upon the coral mocked him. It watched, but did not see. The eyes were blank, empty, without soul or intelligence.

The mind of Eric John Stark fought, in its alien prison, for sanity.

Berild's voice spoke to him. Her hand was on his shoulder Kynon's shoulder …

"All is well, wild man. Do not fear. Kynon's mind is in your body, still sleeping at my command. And you are Kynon now." It was not an easy thing to accept, but he knew that it was so, and he knew that he had wished it to be so. It was easier to be calm after he turned his back on the other.

Berild took him in her arms and held him until he had stopped shuddering, oddly like a mother with a frightened child. Then she kissed him, smiling, and said,

The first time is hard. I can remember—and that was very long ago." She shook him gently. "Now come. We'll take your body to a place of safety. And then I must tell you all of Kynon's plans for those outside."

She spoke to the thing that lay upon the coral, saying, "Get up," and it rose obediently and followed where Berild led, to a tiny barred niche in a side passage. It made no protest when ii was left, locked safely in.

"Only I can give it back to you," said Berild softly. "Remember that."

Stark said, "I will remember."

He went with Berild to Kynon's quarters in the palace. He sat among Kynon's possessions, clothed in Kynon's flesh, and learned how Kynon's mind had planned to loose a red tide upon the peaceful cities of the Border.

Only a small part of his mind was attentive to this. The rest of it was concerned with the redness of Berild's hair and the warmth of her lips, and with the heady knowledge that it was possible to be alive and young forever.

Never to lose the pride of strength, never to know the dimming sight and failing mind of age. To go on, like a child in an endless playground, with no fear of tomorrow.

It was nearly dawn.

Berild rose. She had told him much, but not the things Fianna had told him, of the secret treachery she had planned with Delgaun. She helped Stark to clothe Kynon's body in the harness of war, with the longsword and the shield and the shining spear. Then she set her lips to his so that his borrowed heart threatened to choke him with its pounding, and her eyes were wondrously bright and beautiful.

"It is time," she whispered.

She walked beside him, as he had seen her beside Kynon in Valkis, stepping like a queen.

They came out of the palace, onto the steps where Luhar had died. There were beasts waiting, trapped for war, and an escort of tall chiefs, with pipers and drummers and link-boys to light the way.

Stark mounted Kynon's beast. It sensed the wrongness in him, hissing and rearing, but he held it down, and imperiously raised his hand.

Throbbing drums and skirling pipes, tossing flames where the link-boys ran with the torches, a clash of metal and a cheer, and Kynon of Shun rode down through the streets of Sinharat to the coral cliffs, with the red-haired woman at his side.

They were waiting.

The men of Kesh and the men of Shun were gathered below cliffs, waiting. Stark led the way, as Berild had told him to, a ledge of coral above them. Delgaun was there, with the outlanders and a handful of Valkisians. He looked tired and

tempered. Stark knew that he had been busy for hours with last-minute preparations.

The first pale rays of dawn broke across the desert. A vast ringing cry went up from the gathered armies. After that there was, silence, a taunt expectant hush.

I here was no fear in Stark now. He was past that. Fear was too small an emotion for what was about to be.

He saw Delgaun's golden eyes, hot with a cruel excitement. He saw Berild's secret triumph in her smile. He looked down upon the warriors, and let the magnificent voice of Kynon ring out across the soundless air.

"There will be no war," he said. "You have been betrayed."

In the moment that was left to him, he confessed the lie of the Rama crowns. And then Berild, who was behind him now, had moved like a red-haired fury to drive her dagger into his heart.

In his own body, Stark might have escaped the blow. But the reflexes of Kynon were not as his. They were swift enough to postpone death—the blade bit deep, but not where Berild had wished it. He turned and caught her by the wrists, and said to Delgaun, "She has betrayed you, too. Freka lies in a coral pit—and I am not Kynon."

Berild tore away from him. She spurred her beast toward the Valkisian. She would have broken past him, through the escort, and up the cliffs to safety in the tunnels under Sinharat. But Delgaun was too quick.

One hand caught in the masses of her hair. She was dragged screaming from the saddle, and even then her screams were not of fear, but of fury. She clawed at Delgaun, and he fell with her to the ground.

The tall chieftains of the escort came forward, but they were dazed, and confused by the anger that was rising in them.

Delgaun's wiry body arched. He flung the woman over the ledge, and what happened to her after that Stark did not see, nor wish to see.

He was shouting again to the barbarians, the tale of Delgaun's treachery.

Behind him on the ledge there was turmoil where Delgaun ran on foot between the beasts, and the outlanders made their try for safety. Below him in the desert, where there had been silence, a great deep muttering was growing, like the first growling of a storm, and the ranks of spears rippled like wheat before the wind.

And Stark felt the slow running out of Kynon's blood inside him, where Berild's dagger stood out from his back.

They had headed Delgaun away from the path up the cliff. The two loose mounts had been caught and held. They had tried to catch Delgaun, but he was light and fast and slipped away from them. Now he broke back, toward Kynon's great beast.

Knock the dying man from the saddle, charge through the milling chieftains, who were hampered by their own numbers in that narrow space …

He leaped. And the arms of Kynon, driven by the will of Eric John Stark, encircled him and held him and would not let him go.

The two men crashed to the ledge. Stark let out one harsh cry of agony, and then was still, his hands locked around the Valkisian's throat, his eyes intent and strange.

Men came up, and he gasped, "He is mine," and they let him be.

Delgaun did not die easily. He managed to get his dagger out, and gashed the other's side until the naked ribs showed through. But once again Stark's mind was free in some dark immensity of its own. He was living again the dream he had in Valkis, and this was the end of the dream. N'Chaka had a grip at last on the demon with yellow eyes that hungered for his life, and he would not let go.

The yellow eyes widened. They blazed, and then they slowly dimmed until the last flicker of life was gone. The strength went out of N'Chaka's hands. He fell forward, over his prey.

Below, on the sand, Berild lay, and her outspread hair was as red as blood in the fiery dawn.

The men of Kesh and the men of Shun flowed, in a resistless tide up over the coral cliffs. The chieftains and the pipers and the link-boys joined them, hunting the outlanders and the wolves of Valkis through the streets of Sinharat.

Unnoticed, a dark-haired girl ran down the path to the ledge.

She bent over the body of Kynon, pressing her hand to its heart. Tears ran down and mingled with the blood.

A low, faint moan came from the man's lips. Weeping like a bull, Fianna drew a tiny vial from her girdle and poured three drops of pale liquid on the unresponsive tongue.

XII

HE HAD COME A LONG WAY. HE HAD BEEN DOWN IN THE DEEP black valleys of the Place of Darkness, and the iron frost was in his bones. He had climbed the bitter mountains where no creature of the Twilight Belt might go and live.

There was light, now. He had been lost and wandering, but he had won back to the light. His tribe, his people would be waiting for him. But he knew that he would never see them.

He remembered, then, with the old terrible loneliness, that they were not truly his people. They had raised him, but they were not of his blood.

And he remembered also that they were dead, slain by the miners who had needed all the water of the valley for themselves. Slain by the miners who had taken N'Chaka and put him in a cage.

With a start of terror, he thought he was again in that cage, with the leering bearded faces peering in at him. But in the blinding dazzle of light he could see no bars.

There was only one face. The anxious, pitying face of a girl.

Fianna.

His brain began to clear. Memory returned bit by bit, the fragments fitting themselves gradually into place.

Kynon. Delgaun. Berild. Sinharat, the Ever-Living.

He remembered now with perfect clarity that he was dying, and it seemed a terrible thing to die in the body of another man. For the first time, fully, he felt the separation from his own flesh. It seemed a blasphemous thing, more terrible than death.

Fianna was weeping. She stroked his hair, and whispered, "I am so glad. I was afraid—afraid you would never wake."

He was touched, because he knew that she loved him and would be sad. He lifted his hand to touch her face, to comfort her.

He saw the fingers of that hand, dark against her cheek. Dark… His own fingers. His own hand.

He was not on the ledge. He was back in the coral crypt beneath the palace. The light that had dazzled his eyes was not the sun, but only the flare of torches.

He sat up, his heart pounding wildly.

Kynon of Shun lay beside him on the coral. He was quite dead, his head encircled by a crown of fire, his side open to the white bone where Delgaun's blade had struck.

The wound that Kynon himself had never felt.

The golden coffer was open. The second crown lay near Fianna, with the rod beside it.

Stark looked at her, deep into her eyes. Very softly he said, "I would not have dreamed it."

"You will understand, now—many things," she said. "And I was glad of my power today, because I could truly give you life!" She rose, and he saw that she was very tired. Her voice was dull, as though it counted over old things that no longer mattered.

"You see why I was afraid. If they had ever suspected that I, too, was of the Twice-Born … Berild or Delgaun, each alone, I might have destroyed, but I could not destroy both of them. And if I had, there was still Kynon. You did what I could not, Eric John Stark."

"Why were you against them, Fianna? How were you proof against the poison that made them what they were?"

She answered angrily, "Because I am weary of evil, of scheming for power and shedding the blood of men as though they were sheep! I am not better than Berild was. I, too, have lived a long time, line, and my hands are not clean. But perhaps, by what you helped me do, I have made up a little for my sins."

She paused, her thoughts turned darkly inward, and it was strange to see the shadow of age touching her sweet young face. Then she said, very slowly, like an old, old woman speaking, "I am weary of living. No matter where I go, I am a stranger. You can understand that, though not so well as I. There is an end pleasure, and after that only loneliness is left.

"I have remembered that I was human once. That is why I set myself against their plan of empire. After all these ages I have come round full circle to the starting point, and things seem to me now as they seemed then, before I was tempted by the Sending-on of Minds.

"It's is a wicked thing!" she cried suddenly. "Against nature and the gods, and it has never brought anything but evil!" She caught up the rod and held it in her hands.

"This is the last," she said. "Cities die, and nations perish, and material things, even such as these, are destroyed. One by one the Twice-Born have perished also, through accident or swift disease or murder, as Berild would have slain Delgaun. Now only this, and I, are left."

Quite suddenly, she flung the rod against the coral, and it broke in a cloudy flame and a tinkling of crystal shards. Then, one by one, she broke the crowns.

She stood still for a long moment. Then she whispered, "Now only I am left."

Again there was silence, and Stark was shaken by the magnitude of the thing that she had done. Her slim girl's body somehow took on the stature of a goddess.

After a while he went to her and said awkwardly, "I have not thanked you, Fianna. You brought me here, you saved me ..." "Kiss me once , then," she answered, and raised her lips to his.

"For I love you, Eric John Stark—and that is the pity of it. Because I am not for you, nor for any man."

He kissed her, very tenderly, and there was the bitter taste of tears on her soft lips.

"Now come," she whispered, and took his hand.

She led him back through the labyrinth, into the palace, and then out again into the streets of Sinharat. Stark saw that it was sunset, and that the city was deserted. The tribes of Kesh and Shun had broken camp and gone.

There was a beast ready for him, supplied with food and water. Fianna asked him where he wished to go, and pointed the way to Tarak.

"And you?" he asked. "Where will you go, little one?"

"I have not thought." She lifted her head, and the wind played with her dark hair. She did not smile, and yet suddenly Stark knew that she was happy.

"I am free of a great burden," she whispered. "I shall stay here for a while, and think, and after that I shall know what to do. But whatever it is there will be no evil in it, and in the end I shall rest."

He mounted, and she looked up at him, with a look that wrung his heart although it was not sad.

"Go now," she said, "and the gods go with you."

"And with you." He bent and kissed her once again, and then rode away, down to the coral cliffs.

Far out on the desert he turned and looked back, once, at the white towers of Sinharat rising against the larger moon.

THE END

About the Author

Leigh Douglass Brackett was born December 7th, 1915 in Los Angeles, California. Considered the 'Queen of Space Opera', Brackett was first published in her mid-20s in *Astounding Science Fiction* and was very prolific from the outset. She wrote in different genres; her novel *No Good From a Corpse*, a hard-boiled mystery, led to the second phase of her writing career as a screenwriter, working with William Faulkner on *The Big Sleep*. She married writer Edmond Hamilton in 1946, and the couple nurtured and inspired each other, establishing two strong and entirely separate careers in science fiction writing.

Returning to SF in the '50s, Brackett's planetary adventures grew in length and complexity, as in *The Sea-Kings of Mars*. Brackett's greatest creation of that era was Eric John Stark, an earthman raised on Mercury, who proceeds to have adventures across the solar system. His first apprearance was in *Queen of the Martian Catacombs*.

She returned to TV and film writing in the '60s and '70s, penning westerns starring John Wayne, and Robert Altman's adaptation of Raymond Chandler's *The Long Goodbye*, and the first draft of *The Empire Strikes Back*, which was to be her last work before dying from cancer in 1978.

Leigh Brackett was a pioneer for women in the genre, often unchallenged for her writing. The skill, intricacy, & diversity of her writing projects established an admiration and acceptance among her peers that many women writers struggled to achieve.